The Back Burner

&

Other Stories

By Mary Letts

First published by Lulu.com, 2008

Copywright© Mary Letts 2008

ISBN 978-0-9556929-1-8

For my husband and my three sons,
with many thanks to Caroline and
Tracey for all their help and encouragement.

Janet West

E verything about her cried out that she was the sensible type. Not a Jezebel, not even a romantic like most other visitors to the Greek islands, who indulged in the sentimental notion that the land still belonged in a strange and mystical way to the Ancient world. That classical world where beautiful but fractious gods and goddesses sometimes playfully disguised themselves as humble fishermen (or goatherds, or nowadays leering waiters in the local taverna) for the sole purpose of seducing ripe young mortals.

These more typical tourists headed straight for the soft sand of the beach where their toes could be tickled by the gentle lick of wavelets, and skimmed through their holiday paperbacks of passion or adventure whilst acquiring the perfect tan. But at every convenient paragraph break their eyes would skate off the page to surreptitiously eye the talent from behind the dark lenses of designer sun glasses, breathlessly waiting for one of those rapacious gods or goddesses in disguise to pick them up. But divinity always was a difficult thing to recognise, and - on a Greek island in particular – absolutely no shortage of pretenders to it.

Janet never went near the beach. Her body was not something to be paraded in a thong or bikini. It was simply a sturdy machine to house vital organs in, so as to pump the blood to her brain. And it was certain she had a brain, for no-one would take Macaulay's History of England as their holiday read if they were a mere plodder. What people could *not* work out though, after the event, was whether she had cunning to the same degree as she had intelligence…

Whilst those others so frivolously fried themselves on the beach she spent her time going for rambling walks in the hills, visiting ruins and soaking up the atmosphere of antiquity. Or collecting bunches of wild thyme and listening to the tinkling of the goats' bells as they foraged for the elusive clumps of brittle grass with such dangerously sharp blades they could slice a finger to the bone. It might have been on one of these walks that she first met Doug, who at that time could still manage a modest stroll along the cliff-top path to the dizzy heights of the headland, where a stunningly positioned roofless rectangle of tall fluted columns formed the famous ruined Temple of Artemis.

He had to support himself with a shepherd's crook, one of a hundred identical ones that were stashed in a pot in the village tourist shop and sold for a few drachmas, but could otherwise still walk unaided.

Doug had been on the island for three or four months before Janet arrived; long enough for most of the foreign residents to reach some unkind conclusions about him. He too, but in a different way to Janet, fell outside the mould of the usual longer term visitor because he was neither a would-be artist nor a wannabe writer, nor even a professor enjoying a lazy sabbatical. He had rented one of the five elegant houses in the village; houses that through their size and nobility stood out from the higgledy-piggledy mass of whitewashed, flat-roofed dwellings that clustered round the bay peering eagerly out to sea, hoping that on a very clear day they might defy the laws of physics and for once miraculously catch a glimpse of the distant island of Crete.

These five houses had been stylishly built in the sixteenth century for wealthy Turkish shipbuilders. At that time the island was still smothered in pine trees and the low reefs of rocks alongside the bay provided natural berths for the boats. They had been cleverly sculpted out into smooth, dry dock areas where the pine trunks could be soaked, curved and lashed together to form the hulls.

The fact that he had rented such a house for six months demonstrated that *one* of his claims must be true - that he *genuinely* had money. The fact that he was American was also true - it was immediately self evident. But the less plausible aspects to his biographical tales consisted of the extraordinary numbers of brilliant things he had done (which could only be cross-checked by extensive researches on Wall Street - and who could be bothered?), the dangerous exploits he had undertaken (which only the CIA could confirm), and the very unfortunate and very, *very* rare disease he had recently fallen prey to. It was hopelessly incurable, so his doctor had apparently prescribed one last, relaxing holiday on the Mediterranean by way of swan-song because the poor man had only a few months to live.

It cannot be hard to guess at the reputation he gradually acquired. Whereas he was initially eagerly invited to social events like drinks or dinner parties; later it was only if an extra unaccompanied man were needed to make up the numbers or correct the gender imbalance; until eventually, by the time Janet came to the island, he was altogether shunned. He had become a complete social pariah.

> "Either he's a compulsive liar," people opined, "or just a sad specimen who tells utter porkies to make himself interesting. *'About to die...'* I mean *c'mon,* what kind of a bloody obvious plea for sympathy is that?!"

Harmless white lies would have been no problem. It was quite common for people to fictionalize their past a little, massaging it into a more enticing glow. It was in fact one of the advantages of living an ex-pat life on a remote island that no annoying little rat from your childhood school was likely to pop out of the woodwork and pour cold water on your untrue tales of youthful derring-do. But the skill was keeping these embellishments in proportion, whereas Doug had taken things way too far. He seemed blind to the irritation he caused, the offence in fact. Such ridiculously tall stories insulted his audience's intelligence and played them for suckers. If he meant to gain sympathy from having his fatal illness and admiration for his list of achievements his plan backfired; all he grew to attract was undiluted contempt.

Janet aroused no such violent, negative feelings. She seemed true to herself, made no attempt to project a false image and neither boasted nor complained. Just got on with her life in a steady, solitary, placid way. People regarded her - if they thought about her at all at this stage - as a sturdy, sexless woman with a reliable temperament and a steady mind. They of course pitied her a little for her absence of physical charms: her chunky body, straight, mouse coloured hair, expressionless eyes and large, sensible hands - suitable for rolling the paper thin strips of pastry used in sticky, sugary baclava perhaps, or for turning the endless pages of Macaulay, but most certainly *not* for massaging a well-toned male body. A few people idly suggested she might go in for massaging the odd female one, now and again, but there was no evidence to suggest she did. Just the mindless cliché that every dowdy woman is sure to be a lesbian.

When they were first seen walking back to the village together it was greeted with sage nodding and a knowing chuckle. *Of course,* people whispered, they were kind of *made for each other.* He grown desperate for an audience, *any* audience, and hardly Adonis himself with his weirdo checked shorts, baggy T-shirts and pink freckled neck beneath an embarrassingly awful baseball cap. It presumably gave him the chance to tone down his old stories and try once again with edited, improved versions that did not overstep the bounds of credulity, for she must be the only person on the whole island not to have indulged in gossip, and therefore not to have been warned of his reputation as a charlatan. And, without any prior experience of a man, she would not even recognise the falsities. On top of which, having never been flattered or adored before, she could easily have her normally solid judgment blown away by a few crafty compliments.

Although they were still not invited to dinner an element of diluted goodwill did go out to them. People began to observe their companionship *almost* fondly, imagining her clucking like an old hen over his infirmities, and in exchange him buttering her up with sentimental fluff and nonsense. Perhaps they discussed the lesser known Greek Myths and the admirable matter of fact-ness of Macaulay, who knows? It did seem that he began to hobble more obviously, and lean against her more heavily where the path was particularly stony and uneven, and perhaps they grew less ambitious about reaching a specific goal like the Temple of Artemis in the course of their outings, but this was put down to a deepening mutual affection and his need for constant mothering. No-one seriously thought it signified deteriorating health.

Also, it was assumed he only looked paler by contrast to her, for her endlessly sensible lifestyle without alcoholic excess and with plenty of fresh air and exercise had at last brought a ruddy colour to her pallid cheeks, so that she almost looked healthy - but still remarkably sexless and plain of course.

Their friendship had been chugging along in a companionable way (it was never assumed to be remotely raunchy or sexual) for maybe a month or so when it was suddenly noticed they had gone! No explanations, no goodbyes, no fanfare; they had simply left the island as quietly as they came. Rumour suggested they had gone together, but based on guesswork rather than certain knowledge. Perhaps he had run out of money to rent the Turkish house; or she had finally come to the end of Macaulay; or they had gone to choose him a coffin; - these were the kind of quips that went the rounds.

A further month and news that they had married filtered through. It seemed out of character for Janet to take such a major step so precipitously - she could only have known the man for less than four months after all, so there was the feeling she had been *had* in some vague way. Duped, poor ugly duckling, bowled over by the first bit of male attention she ever had - or was ever likely to have. How *could* a sensible person like her listen to his impossible, implausible yarns with a straight face? How did she tolerate him launching into those awful medical and hospital stories and hear him boast about the statistical rarity of his disease (it afflicted one in four thousand trillion or

4

something!) with its ridiculous name no-one had ever heard of let alone knew how to pronounce, without collapsing in derision?

> "He was always on about getting married," Phyllis remembered. "Kept saying it was such a waste for someone with his wealth to die a bachelor. What'd he do with the millions? If he left it 'em charity he'd be fretting throughout the afterlife that they'd been frittered away at the admin stage! He asked *me* first, - then he tried it on with Chloe. And Sandra after that."

> "Not really," Sandra frowned as she tried to remove the last obstinate patches of skin from what looked to be a divinely ripe fig. "He knew I wasn't having it. Silly moo, falling into his trap... I wonder if she knew he'd already asked so many of us?"

> "Perhaps she just needed someone to mother. Then he came on a plate, without all the bother of using a man and the effort of pregnancy."

As winter closed in on the island and the flow of tourists shrank to a dribble, the subject of Doug and Janet receded from people's minds. The winter season was one of collective introspection for the caiques were at the mercy of the sea storms and sometimes could not sail for days on end, so the island was cut off and this added to its changed character. In summer it was a resplendent jewel set in a deep blue sea, an island of daydreams. In winter it shrank to a giant slab of dark rock amidst turbulent waters, sometimes half submerged by the violent waves and on most days relentlessly pummelled by fierce winds as if it were a punch bag at the mercy of an iron fist.

Home life retreated forlornly indoors, for the patios were wild wind tunnels filled with jostling leaves and the curling dead brown flowers of once crimson bougainvillea, while the outside tables became so encrusted with layers of salt whipped off the sea by the horizontal pressure of the wind that even on a calm day no-one could be bothered to scrape it off and set them for lunch. Evenings were spent huddled in front of log fires and, more likely than not, afternoons worrying about the diminishing stash of firewood. Should more be ordered? Should a stroll be taken into the mountains to collect the trunks of fallen pine trees? Or down to the beach to gather kindling from the scatterings of driftwood pitched onto the pebbles?

The rain, although less frequent than the wind, was every bit as forceful. It lashed down with such venom it stung the skin like a tattooist's needles and seemed determined to strip the bark off trees and scrub the whitewash from the walls of houses. It formed torrents that gurgled and thundered down the narrow cobbled streets, and the village boys who were still light enough not to sink a wooden tray if they sat on it could hurtle down and pretend to be white water rafting.

Eventually the winter gave way to an early but uncertain spring, then thousands of crocus-like flowers blossomed in bright yellow clusters on the hillsides. The warmer sunshine activated the sharp tang of pine resin and the sky and sea turned from grey to hesitant blue, the goatherds led the goats out into the mountain pastures and once more the tinkle of their bells was carried on the light breeze. Three weeks' old baby goats gambolled on spindly legs beside their mothers, suckling at every opportunity.

For a solid week the noises of whitewashing dominated the village; the slurping of liquids, the clanging of buckets, the soft, swishing sound of fat brushes making sweeping strokes over the walls, and the low murmur of conversations from male and female voices - for this was one of those rare tasks the men and women shared. By the end of the week the village was transformed from a bedraggled collection of rain-stained, grubby grey houses into a fragmented prism of pure, blinding white light. Blinding, that is, to all but immortal eyes.

Another tourist season, another summer. The donkeys were led out from winter stables or walled corals to have their mucous-filled eyes cleaned up with cotton wool dabbed in bicarbonate of soda, while their matted, dung-smeared coats were hosed down, then strenuously brushed and combed until they nearly gleamed. They were the means by which the older or infirm tourists were transported up the steep cliff path to the Temple of Artemis, even though some were so small that their riders' legs, despite the high peaked saddles and bulky cushions piled on top to prevent the pinching of a tourist's behind, virtually touched the stony ground. Rumour had it that Charlton Heston, when he visited the island long ago, had hired the customary donkey for the Temple trip but felt so sorry when it trembled under his weight (and height) that he ended up carrying it on *his* back! Incidentally it did not escape village notice that Doug, instead of leaning so heavily against the bulk of Janet, *could* have leased a donkey to carry him about and thus honoured village tradition, but *naturally* he had claimed an allergy to donkey hairs. (And some said his aversion to donkeys was due to the disrespectful way they drowned him out by braying dementedly at his stories).

A steady trickle of tourists filtered into the village from the harbour town to the north, and the tourist shop changed back into a tourist shop after a winter selling vegetables.

It was then that the whisperings about Janet began to circulate. Her sister Clarissa arrived first, moving in with such pomp and splendour to the Turkish house that Doug had rented the previous summer that it could only mean the house had been bought rather than rented this time around. Clarissa was completely different to Janet. Perhaps she was a half-sister, not a full sibling; or Janet had taken her genes from one parent and Clarissa the other. They bore no resemblance either physically or temperamentally, or - it has to be said - intellectually, for since Clarissa had inherited all the looks and sensuality she had not felt any obligation to develop her higher cerebral functions. (Or, if she had, they were long ago drowned in drugs). The one thing they *did* seem to share, however, was a sudden pot of good fortune, for although Clarissa knew no-one in the resident ex-pat community and divulged little background information, she made it known that her sister Janet would soon be coming to supervise the full makeover of the old house that was now hers in perpetuity. Nothing was gleaned about Doug, but it was assumed he would be coming with her.

"D'you reckon she's inherited some *real* money then?" Rudi, Chloe's current German boyfriend asked, with a note that Chloe irritably recognised as wistfulness.

"Prob'ly," she replied. "That'd at least explain what attracted Doug - apart from the brainy discussions they kept having, that is. Even *he* wasn't quite as ugly a specimen as her, and at least his loony stories showed he had imagination," and she gave Rudi a peevishly accusatory stare.

Next to arrive was Clarissa's boyfriend called (for some reason) Rand. Whatever the reason, it was *not* that he was a filthy rich Afrikaner with money robbed from the gold and diamond mines of South Africa, since his accent was neither Durban nor Cape Town but downmarket London. He was even lazier than Clarissa - if that were possible. Her slow and ready smile of satisfaction when she hit the streets at midday suggested, in fact, that his name was most likely an abbreviation of Randy, and the lucky girl seemed to be indulging in an indolent life of unlimited sex *and* money.

Once again there were flickerings of concern about poor ugly Janet, who now had a couple of humping, sluggish parasites living off her as well as all the nursing duties Doug would demand. People did not seem to spot the illogical side to this argument, for if she had inherited parental or family money, Clarissa would surely have received an equal share and - apart from her ultra-indolent lifestyle - could not therefore be accused of living off Janet. It would simply mean two sisters sharing a house with their respective partners, and Janet merely put upon through being easily the most intelligent, practical and energetic of the outfit.

Clarissa adored colour to the same degree Janet loved plainness. She splashed out liberally on swathes upon swathes of raw, creamy Greek cotton and as many bales of fine Thai silk, because her one energetic activity (apart from the sex) was sewing. The neighbours frequently heard a humming, whirring noise at odd hours of the night; a mechanical sound distinct from the more varied rhythms and melodies of sexual pleasure, and before long both she and the curtains were as delightfully draped as exotic birds of paradise. Clarissa had such a charming smile she could melt even the sternest villager's disapproval, and she soon needed maximum charm to overcome her serious faux-pas of taking a ferry boat to the Turkish mainland to buy rugs for the house, on the grounds that it was, after all, a Turkish house. Newly painted interiors, freshly hung curtains and traditional Turkish rugs completed her contribution to its thorough refurbishment. At last the stage was set for Janet's return.

"She'll hate it I tell you," Sandra declared, after she had persuaded Clarissa to show her around. "It's kind of Ikea, oriental style! She'll want everything back to plain white again. And Rand just lopes about in this silk loin cloth looking utterly depraved.

"Too much sex," Chloe glanced regretfully at Rudi.

"*And* drugs," Sandra surmised. "The back patio's a vast marijuana plantation - or will be come summer when they're fully grown. At the moment they're only tiddly seedlings."

"Any news of Doug?"

"Sorry, didn't ask. I keep forgetting you were interested in him."

"Oh pack it in! *Not* interested - just curious. I bet he thought when he told all those stories he'd never come back here again. He can't possibly have expected to join forces with someone who'd end up buying a house here."

Three days later Janet arrived, very low key. She stayed at home for the first few days, so that whether her parent's legacy plus nearly an added year of life and the demands of caring for Doug had changed her were unknowns and therefore the subject of mild speculation. Only the village electrician and the man who professed some knowledge of plumbing saw the insides of the house, and they said nothing beyond it being '*policala*'.

A swimming pool was apparently at the planning stage. If so, it would be the very first in the village. Up until now no-one had contemplated such wasteful luxury because the golden half-moon of the beach and the bright blue expanse of the Mediterranean shivered enticingly a mere two minutes' walk downhill, costing a convenient nothing to maintain. Still, people reasoned, with a body like hers it must be more comfortable exposing it in privacy; maybe she never ventured to the beach but always went walking before because she was too shy to strip off in public. Doug too, being something of an invalid, might need to swim for therapeutic reasons. He had already found the walk to the rocks a strain last autumn.

But if the swimming pool was to be built before the end of the summer then Rand's marijuana plantation would have to be transplanted with all concomitant risks; it was an interesting dilemma for outsiders - because it would reveal which sister *really* held the reins of power.

The next development sent ripples of excitement through the ex-pat community. A house warming party was afoot - with an open door policy on guests, so even those who had snubbed Doug (everyone!) need not fear exclusion. *Now* was the chance to satisfy curiosity on a great many counts, so the intervening days passed unbearably sluggishly.

When the evening came the cobbled alleyway approaching the house exuded a soft and subtle welcome. The village had only recently converted from 120 to 240 volts, with *literally* hair raising consequences! Despite the warning letters sent in duplicate to all householders very few bothered to read them, or, if they did, still fewer bothered to comply with their instructions. Not altogether their fault, of course, since many an ex-pat struggled to properly understand them, their comprehension of written Greek being even worse than their spoken. The wiring in most houses was therefore still unearthed, and consequently lethal.

On the day of the switchover squawks of surprise and screams of agony could be heard from all over as the simple act of switching on a bathroom light or plugging in a kettle sent agonising voltage searing up arms, through chests, down legs. By the end of the day the tally of injuries embraced burns, shocks, traumas, bitten tongues, one epileptic seizure, three heart attacks and - miraculously - merely one fatality. Two people greatly benefited from the change: the village electrician, who was suddenly viewed with massively increased respect - more than the equivalent boost in voltage, and the small fishing/diving shop, because the sales of rubber boots and rubber wetsuits to insulate against electric shocks fairly skyrocketed.

The bright new street lights were universally hated. Previously the village had been lit by gentle lamps that glowed as softly as candles, leaving pleasant shadows where lovers could kiss and canoodle in privacy, and a drunk man could safely risk relieving himself without his floodlit shadow alerting the local policeman (public urination was strictly illegal) as he stumbled back

9

home. The only powerful exterior lighting used then was directed upwards at the ruined Temple of Artemis, so that it eerily resembled a row of dinosaur legs that had fused into the clifftop rock during some geological eruption aeons ago.

Now, however, the blinding power of the new street lights so mesmerized the eyes that the distant floodlighting of the Temple faded to invisibility. There were no shadows left, and even children's faces looked wizened and old in the harsh glare.

So, to achieve this soothing, welcoming atmosphere in the final approach the Janet-Clarissas had artfully contrived to switch off the offensive new streetlight and replace it with two subdued gas flares mounted like ancient torches on the stone wall. The main entrance door stood open whilst soft, enticing music played within…

The interior lighting was equally subtle. Pinpricks of light twinkled like stars from crevices in the immense stone wall that ran the full length of the house, while there were old bronze candelabra, wrought iron table lamps and elegant standing lamps giving off different shades of gold, orange and creamy light so that the full moon shining directly down into the cobbled courtyard looked oddly bland and out of place. It was probably the lighting more than the décor that had evoked Ikea for Sandra.

Two long trestle tables groaned beneath the weight of whole spit-roasted goats, a mountain of spicy lamb kebabs, dolmades, zadziki, taramasalata, five different varieties of olives and many more different types and shapes of bread. The food had been prepared and transported from the Turkish restaurant in the harbour town to the north, and this would have deeply offended the villagers, especially the owner of the local taverna, had they received the news secondhand. However Janet had tactfully invited them all, and once they actually tasted the food their mouths watered and their complaints and churlish thoughts melted, and they happily toasted the house and its new occupants with fine Retzina and cloudy glasses of ouzo, all of it local to the island. Clarissa and Rand were dressed like Barbary pirates, and every so often Rand would flourish his cutlass to slice off another dozen servings of roasted goat.

Intriguingly, Janet was nowhere to be seen for the early stages of hellos, welcoming kisses and first drinks, but once the atmosphere was nicely warmed she chose her moment to descend the staircase from the masterbedroom above the vaulted entrance hall.

She had not grown noticeably older, more affluent or more beautiful (or less ugly as the spiteful would phrase it) but there was a quiet dignity about her now, a new sense of power and determination. She might not inspire admiration (and certainly not any lusting), but at the same time she no longer aroused pity. And the fear she would very soon engender would not be long emerging...

"Doug's not coming down to join us then?" someone made bold to ask her several minutes later, after the obligatory pleasantries and lashings of compliments about house and food had been gone through.

A faint shadow of regret seeped into her expression, but she quickly recovered and answered with a faintly ironic smile.

"Hardly. Though I think he'd be bowled over by the assumption he's 'up there' as you put it," and her eyes flicked dramatically heavenward, "because he always said he was a definite candidate for 'down under'. But in the five months since he died he's not made one ghostly reappearance."

Only those in the immediate vicinity overheard the news of his death, but within minutes it travelled back and forth like Chinese whispers, and the yawning black cavities of their ignorance began to oppress them. Could they, *could they really* have all got it horribly wrong? The seeds of self-doubt began to swell, but not yet burst into vibrant life. What's she saying? What was that? Ssh, I'm trying to listen...

"No, obviously it came as no surprise. He knew exactly what to expect, his doctor never stinted with the truth. We couldn't have been more prepared, really. Even though the reality of death is always a shock, no matter how much you're expecting it."

"Well, he would have loved that, but it didn't happen. The disease - I'm afraid I never can get the Chinese pronunciation right - was named after the first man to contract it, and even though Doug's was a variation of the normal characteristics, if you can use the word *normal* for something so incredibly rare, his strain wasn't named after him despite his pleas. - Just the unpronounceable name, and then *by proxy.*"

"Sorry, I didn't quite catch your question there. Are you OK? You're looking rather pale all of a sudden."

"Ha!" she laughed merrily, "No, it doesn't embarrass me remotely to be so rich! I've got plenty of business ideas and I'll spread it around, set up Foundations and sponsorships and the like. At least I can use Doug's name for *them*, to make up for his disappointment it wasn't used for the virus. I'm setting up cotton mills and clothing outlets on the island - it'll keep

Clarissa's hands busy because she'll be the main designer. She's no good with Rand because she prefers him naked to clothed, so her heart's not in the fall of the material."

No-one, afterwards, found the heart to gossip. The ensuing days passed in subdued silence while each, from the safe seclusion of their private shells, mulled over what had happened and very gradually and painfully came to terms with it.

It felt like missing out on the lottery when your habitual numbers come up, but on the one and only occasion in several successive years that you failed to enter it. That was the financial angle, but even more insidious was the emotional fallout. With the emotions, unlike the electrical shocks at the time of voltage change, there was no rubberised armoury to insulate against the pain. It flooded through them in waves; waves of self-hate and disgust at their skewered misunderstandings; disbelief followed by rage and succeeded by deep depression that they had got it all so exactly and perfectly wrong.

Their misreading of Doug held up many mirrors to their meanness, and the laughter they had expended on him returned to echo maniacally in their ears, but at least that had finality. Doug was dead and would never be coming back 'I told you so-*ing*'.

The real, incurable suffering was the effect Janet had on them, and from that there was no escape since she seemed to be planning to stay for ever. From a mousy nobody she now held almost divine power over them, for although everyone wondered if she had known all along that Doug would die and all she had to get through was a brief three month spell of mothering and nursing and she would then be free and the owner of an immense fortune, nobody dared ask her. They even wondered, secretly and silently to themselves, if she might not have hastened his death once he became too weak to resist a fly.

In truth the feeling she now inspired was not pity at all, but a dreadful blend of awe and fear.

The Neighbour's Cat

Whenever the river flooded the adjoining fields were so low-lying and level that the water, once it breached the river banks, submerged them in the blink of an eye. Seconds later it was already lapping at the roots of the beech hedge that bordered Douglas' garden.

With every flood nature had to rapidly readjust. There was a well orchestrated - but presumably also panic-stricken - retreat by the whole mole community, and next day neat clusters of mole hills would pop up along the shores of this newly created lake like a huge encampment of earthy tepees, its mole-builders having enterprisingly burrowed through a quarter of a mile of thick clay soil. It testified to an immense mole population whose existence was almost forgotten the rest of the year. Plus there must have been many more who had failed to survive this emergency journey.

The worms then began heaving up the immaculate smoothness of Douglas' velvety lawn with their endless chewing, digesting and expelling, while those birds whose usual habitat was now underwater would cunningly hunt along this new, temporary shoreline, scooping them up like so much pale pink spaghetti.

It was like evolution switched to fast forward. Some adapted and flourished; others perished. It was also stunningly beautiful, because the outer reaches of the lake had a mirror-like calm that reflected the lightness of the sky and drained the darkness from the winter landscape, as if one were living in a slender world suspended between two skies. The only visible turbulence was close in to the original course of the river, where the force of the current and powerful undertow created ripples and circular eddies as it pulled the water back, determined it should not forget its true river identity and its watery purpose of returning to the sea.

Living beside a river is a lesson in humility. Land you *think* you own proves the illusory nature of such possession, for water can swallow it in seconds. And whilst you remain impotently stranded on a bank in a single spot as if forgotten by the passage of time, the river flows by regardless, a perpetual reminder of the past from which it has arisen, and the future into which it will flow. It transmits a melancholy spirit of insecurity, of endless impermanence.

These, anyway, were the philosophical thoughts that wandered through Douglas' mind as he trudged across the now marshy swamplands after the floods had retreated - less neatly than they had arrived, leaving outlying puddles distastefully edged with yellow scum and trails of broken twigs, torn flower stalks and sodden autumn leaves spread across the flattened grass of the fields.

He tried to imagine the massive devastation of a huge flooded river in tropical lands fed by monsoon rains. Narrowing his eyes into slits he fancied he could actually see the bloated corpses of drowned buffalo and the half-eaten bodies of village dogs and worse; whereas *his* reality yielded nothing more dramatic than a drowned water rat and the flapping body of a trout trapped in a small, fast evaporating puddle, having failed to catch a ride on the last tributary stream flowing back to the river.

His own father had enlisted and experienced the misery of the trenches of World War1. He was killed just before the Armistice, two months before Douglas was born, and somehow Douglas had vicariously absorbed enough horrific images of death in a desolate, mudsoaked landscape not to feel a sudden shiver run down his spine. Deftly he scooped up the flailing body of the trout and carried it in his cupped and sympathetic hands towards a deeper channel of water that still had an outlet to the river, but either from fright or insufficient submergence in water as it leaked through his fingers the fish died before it could be saved. So, on the principles of waste not want not, he popped it in the pocket of his oilskin jacket to grill in the oven for supper. His dog, a long-legged springer spaniel, followed obediently at his heels without bothering to whine for the pocketed catch, for it knew it never had fish due to the dangers of fatally sharp bones.

Douglas did not believe in God and all his hierarchy of angels, cherubim, seraphim and suchlike, and even less in the earthly hierarchy of church authority such as bishops, archbishops, vicars, the Pope, priests or poor molested young choirboys. But he was an ardent respecter of nature and its inbuilt laws. And he liked to feel that a kind of natural order reigned in the world. Of course there were moments of chaos: floods, earthquakes, droughts, volcanic eruptions, big freezes, violent thaws, hurricanes, tornados and thunderous storms, but overall you could rely on nature to restore the balance of bad with good and to maintain the regular beat of time: day, night and the careful progress of seasons. Animal and plant life responded to this, even relied on it. Only humans thought they were above it, could interfere and distort it.

Since his retirement he still saw a small circle of close friends, mainly fellow countrymen who shared his love of rural life. But he had no respect for the mass of humanity or its modern values, nor in pompous politicians who sent men to die in useless wars.

There was, however, one creature he hated above everything - his neighbour's horror of a cat. Although *technically* a furry, four-legged member of the animal species, its behaviour was entirely contrary to nature. It was too arrogant and self-possessed, too downright nasty and destructive. It was, in fact, *such* a devilishly unpleasant piece of work it made him realise that man, although undeniably clever to domesticate co-operative animals like horses, sheep, chicken, cattle and dogs, was totally stupid in attempting to civilise the feline race.

This particular furry fiend had harboured an irrational hatred of him from the very beginning of their acquaintance, roughly four months ago. And ever since then its sole purpose in life had been to get up his nose.

Every night it stalked the nightingale, who now no longer sung melodiously from the lone elm tree overhanging his garage. It deliberately clattered the loose tiles exactly above his bed, then yowled like a banshee as soon as he sunk into a peaceful, dreamless sleep. It had killed the young cherry tree he planted two years ago by sharpening its claws on the trunk, stripping off the bark in sad, curling rolls; and it made a daily ritual of chasing away the friendly robin that perched on the kitchen windowsill while he ate his breakfast. But of course it made no effort at all to discourage the rats who scuffled boldly in and out of his loft!

Its morning constitutional was to circle his garden five times in a casual, provocative way, twitching its tail and glaring, challenging him to accuse it of trespassing so that it could retort that the whole world was its oyster and it was answerable to no-one.

It regularly used his wonderful velvety clover lawn as a lavatory, peeing languidly onto the lushest areas, and just as liberally over the herbaceous border so that every flower wilted and died. It did its other, fouler business by crouching on a different patch of pristine grass, then half-heartedly scratching at a few blades in a pathetic pretence of burying the vile excrement. Every single day he would have to come with a shovel and clear his lawn, and if he ever confronted the cat in flagrante it would stare right through him with pale yellow eyes of hostility, or else close its eyes to altogether blot him out of its superior consciousness.

He had been forced to take counter-measures. First he bought a raucous bird scarer that ratcheted around like an unoiled windmill, but the cat turned deaf ears to it and he had to dismantle it for his own peace. Then he set his dog to chase it away, but the poor thing returned with a deep, bleeding gouge on the bridge of its nose and a severe dent to its confidence. His most recent tactic, which made him feel *almost* ashamed, was to buy a tin of cat food which he doused in the most virulent of rat poisons and left on a plate at the foot of his bird feeder, a spot where the cat enjoyed hanging out so as to taunt the birds who came for crumbs.

Of course the cat was not fooled. It yawned, stretched, performed a lengthy and outrageously sexual toilette, then ate not a single morsel of the death-food! Perhaps it had simply exhausted all available saliva on its backside and had no appetite left. But Douglas felt convinced it had guessed at his murderous intent and deliberately foiled him again, since it sniffed the food and sauntered off in a bored yet knowing manner after treading plumb in the middle of the jellied meat - which jumped off the plate and squelched onto a mossy paving stone.

People joke that dogs resemble their owners, but he now applied that axiom to cats. Or *this* cat, certainly. He did realise, whilst busily engaged in gingerly, ruefully clearing up the squishy pulp of poisoned cat food from the stone flags (for fear the dog would wolf down the poison) that - to any sane, rational observer - his whole dilemma with this cat must appear crazy. Of course he should not be forced to wrack his brains over how to outwit the cat - or for that matter take it on *at all.* Nor should he be losing his dignity cleaning up after it. The common sense approach would be to call on its owner and explain, calmly and rationally, exactly what the cat did that was unacceptable - and would be found unacceptable by anyone (apart from one of those cranky old cat-crazed biddies in their nineties who prowl the city streets at night looking for stray moggies to rescue).

Its owner might well become just such a cat crazed biddy when or *if* she finally reached that over-ripe age, but at present she was a mere forty-something. She *was* already crazed, however, so her cat's behaviour was most probably symptomatic of her whole take on life, and definitely it mirrored her attitude to him. If he was to tell her how sick he was of her cat traipsing all over his garden, killing trees, withering grass, frightening birds, terrorising his dog, bullying him and generally making his life a misery, why, she would only throw back her head and laugh in delight!

She had moved into Damson Cottage approximately four months ago, a transparently obvious townie with no real knowledge or respect for the rhythms of the country. Yet she pretended to be an expert on husbandry; organic this, organic that, 'I plant my peas on a waxing moon and my parsnips on a waning,' she was *that* kind of ex-allotment phoney who thought growing things was *spiritual*. Whereas for Douglas farming and gardening were essentially natural, practical activities; there was no need to mix them up with religion.

In her skewered view animals were more than equal to humans and must be allowed to roam freely and without fear (hence the futility of challenging her cat's movements). They should never be put on a lead, trapped, culled, hunted, shot at or reared for meat. If a tough old goat at the end of its tether (metaphorically, for physically was not allowed in her book) needed to be killed and cooked for a particularly important occasion, then the killing should be done benignly and swiftly with a knife to the throat, not brutally and slowly in a slaughterhouse gadget.

She lived alone with her two kids, a boy and a girl, ages pre-teen but double figured, and Douglas reckoned her unfortunate husband had probably gone through several years of undiluted hell before realising divorce was a viable escape route.

He knew she despised him. Everything about him spelt e-n-e-m-y. He was seventy, so the *wrong* generation; he was a man (or used to be - but ever since his wife died a year and a half ago he had not put his manliness to the test and could no longer swear to it); he kept a dog (an *enslaved* animal); he fished for carp and trout and shot pheasants (*cruel* and *upper-classist*); he had lived in the same house for nearly fifty years (a creature of *habit*, a *stuck-in-the-mud*); and while he still voted Conservative for want of any real alternative she was as *Green* as jealousy itself.

The only thing they might have agreed on if they had ever exchanged a civil word was religion; she being a self-styled pagan and Douglas one in spirit, although he had never acknowledged that specific label.

But all she ever exchanged with him were sporadic comments drenched in sarcasm.

"Off to shoot defenceless birds are we?"

"Sorry - didn't notice how *very red* your neck is."

"*Do* forgive me for lowering the tone of *your* neighbourhood."

"*So sorry* my cat killed your favourite sparrow. Such *unnatural* behaviour."

His retorts had been pathetically feeble, he was ashamed to admit.

Late in the evening on the day after his abortive poisoning attempt, Douglas was sitting in his old, worn leather armchair cleaning his hunting rifle. He prodded a wad of oiled gauze down each barrel so that the cartridge could slide smoothly down it, with lightning and invariably fatal speed. Even though the sharp smell of gun oil evoked many pleasant memories of frosty winter mornings, moist dark earth, bright red berries, and the sweet smell of wood smoke drifting across the valley from the distant beech woods cresting the line of hills beyond the river, deep down he felt dispirited, lonely and old.

Suddenly he heard a scratching, scuffling sound outside. Instinctively he laid aside the cleaning rod to click the gun straight, into correct operating position. Very carefully he then slotted two cartridges down its twin barrels. Killing something was not really in the forefront of his mind, he merely wanted to be prepared. He had half a dozen fluffy young defenceless chickens in the coop near the greenhouse, and had seen a badger's spoor in the hedgerow beside the lane only the day before yesterday.

The scratching sound was definitely coming from the direction of his beech hedge beyond the 'cat's lavatory' end of the lawn. He took the precaution of turning off the overhead light before opening the curtain an inch or two so that he could, hopefully, have a clear view of the source of the noise without being seen himself...

Once his eyes adjusted to the darkness he detected something white struggling through the dense underbelly of the hedge. At first he thought it was the white stripe of a badger's forehead, but as it emerged further he saw that the entire animal was white and fluffy haired. The dreaded neighbour's cat! He never consciously reached a decision. It was as if he were programmed, on auto-pilot, even bewitched! In perfect silence he opened the window with one hand, while with the other he lifted the gun until his two hands could work efficiently in tandem, and one finger pressed against the trigger. He watched and waited while the cat turned two full circles, as if executing a neat pirouette on an unseen lavatory seat. And he continued watching as it squatted on its haunches with its back towards him, obviously satisfied it had found the right spot.

He was even unaware of actually pulling the trigger, but there was no disputing the deafening retort that shattered the silence of the night, and he definitely felt the rebound of the gun pound painfully against his shoulder. He saw the sudden jerk and stutter of the white cat as it catapaulted up into the air, then fell back onto the grass. And lay perfectly still.

He stood by the open window for a while, in a state of shock. He heard the distant shriek of an owl and a dog barking from the direction of the village, and he dreaded the inevitable approaching roar of fury from the neighbour herself, come to curse him in her black lace nightie with her dainty bedroom slippers drenched in dew.

The seconds ticked by, accumulating into minutes; but still nothing happened. Maybe she was watching a crime thriller on TV and the shot had exactly coincided with the gangster shootout in the back streets…or perhaps, from lingering city habits, she always popped wax pellets in her ears so as to blot out the thunder of traffic. Whatever the reason, she did not come, and he at last galvanised himself into action. He *must* get rid of the guilty evidence. He put on his oilskin and rubber boots, found an old dusty sack in the garage, grabbed the gardening spade and crossed the dewy grass to the motionless white shape on the lawn.

Again, he was unaware of actually making a decision. He could have dug a hole in his herbaceous border, the earth was not so frost riven as to make this impossible, but he did not. Instead he shovelled up the body, still warm and flexible, and slung it distastefully into its hessian-coffin. Then he set off across the field towards the river with the sack slung over his shoulder like some demented Santa Claus.

A paper-thin layer of ice skimmed the floodwater puddles making the walk treacherous, and whenever he jerked because he had nearly lost his footing, or leaned sideways to heave his boot out from the powerful suction of the mud, the cat's sharp claws seemed to jab into his back. He was desperate to get rid of the body as quickly and quietly as possible, but what with the slithering on the ice and the slurping in mud he abandoned stealth and sounded like a wallowing hippopotamus. Also, he was a fool not to have brought his dog, since it was now howling non-stop from the misery of being left out of such an unusual hunting adventure.

At last he reached the footbridge. It was not the closest point between river and house but was easily the safest place in these slippery conditions from which to hurl a sack into the current without following suit. He took a final peek into the sack to ensure the cat had not achieved some Houdini-style escape. Even in death it stared back at him with unmitigated malice in its unseeing eyes. Hurriedly retying the sack he slung it over the parapet, listening on tenterhooks for the splash that was hauntingly magnified in the darkness.

By the time he reached home he felt utterly exhausted. Collapsing into bed still wearing his mud-spattered clothes, he slept as soundly as a baby until well after sunrise.

The next day he did not exactly exult in the cat's death, but he felt a surge of relief that its reign of tyranny was over. The birds too relished their newfound freedom. They chirped loudly and merrily in the branches of the apple tree or hopped confidently across the lawn, and even the robin returned to the kitchen window to check that Douglas' breakfast routine remained the same. The dog's tail wagged continuously, and the cheeky red squirrel once more dared to search for beech nuts along the hedgerow.

That cat had it coming, he reassured himself. But nevertheless he felt a twinge of guilt when he imagined the two children hopelessly searching for it, and he prayed they would not pin up a 'Lost' notice on the tree down the lane that would haunt him horribly.

Five miles downstream the local market town spread its urban sprawl across the same valley, and before the river entered the town it had to pass through a sluice gate. In order to prevent the more serious and costly flooding of the town, whenever the river levels reached a certain height these sluice gates were closed - and this of course was what exacerbated the extent of the flooding upstream.

The gates, closed four days ago as a precautionary measure, had just been partially reopened because the river level had dropped to a margin of safety. Two men in orange oilskin jackets were closely monitoring the flow of water through the narrow, partial barrier, because the town was inordinately proud of the new aesthetic facelift it had given to the previously downtrodden riverside zone. Impressive brick walkways had been built, and curved footbridges, picnic tables, benches and modernistic flowerbeds - so they were desperately anxious not to have folks' aesthetic sensibilities offended by the site of unpalatable detritus from the flood floating through it. The sort of thing these two men were meant to be on the lookout for, therefore, were the revoltingly bloated bodies of flood drowned animals. They had already hawked out two dead sheep, a legless heron, eight pigeons and a mangled otter caught in a snare.

"Comin' your side Fred - a sack with somethin' in it."

"Right yer'are."

Fred, after a slight struggle, managed to successfully hook out the sack that had been already snagged and torn a number of times by branches and the sharp piers of bridges.

"I 'ope it 'ain't one of them stillborn babies, like we 'ad last time," Fred muttered as he struggled awkwardly with the wet string.

Douglas had not thought to check the cat's neck before dumping it in the sack, unwisely assuming its owner kept to her strict principles of no collars or leads. In fact it wore a flea collar, attached to which was a disc with her address and telephone number. It was patently obvious from its brutally butchered backside how this cat met its death, so the two men, assuming the owner to be the perpetrator of the dirty deed, were somewhat incensed that he or she had been too damn' lazy to bury the corpse as custom demanded, instead having risked the health and hygiene of others by dumping it in the river as if it were some public floating waste disposal chute. The tone of their telephone call was decidedly unpleasant. She could bloody collect the thing *right pronto* or be sprung a hefty fine for illegal river dumping.

The fact that a local reporter was there when she breezed in to take possession of the body was not her doing. It was actually Fred's fault.

"It's a snotty female. Townie with a toff's voice an' a toffee-nosed attitude. Let's give her a bit of negative publicity, shall we? Thinkin' she can throw old pets in the river when she's 'ad enough of 'em, not caring 'ow much they stink out others."

But she was nobody's fool either. She could read anger in a man's voice as well as any recent divorcee, so she sensibly brought both children along when she came to collect the body - and no doubt had some pungent ready-peeled onions hidden in her handbag. She had no trouble at all convincing the local reporter how shocked, devastated and distraught all three of them were at the sight of their dear, dead, much-loved pet; and their acting skills were not put under much strain in any case because the cat truly did look terrible after spending sixteen hours submerged in muddy water.

"Oh, how *could* he?" she sobbed into her lavender scented handkerchief, "poor Sheba, my poor, darling Sheba. Shot to pieces and drowned as well, just to bloody rub it in!"

"You...you know who shot it then?" the reporter asked her gently, not wishing to have left the comfort of the local pub for no story whatsoever.

"Like hell I do," she growled, almost overdoing the switch from grief to aggression. "It's my bastard of a bloody neighbour, he's always out shooting poor defenceless animals. I knew he hated darling Sheba's guts but I never thought he'd go *this* far."

"So, what's his name?" and the reporter began scribbling furiously in his little child's exercise book, ironically at almost exactly the same time as Douglas was inwardly, and of course foolishy, rejoicing at the demise of his feline nemesis..

The first hint Douglas had that his quiet, uneventful, wonderfully secluded existence was about to implode was the sight of a photographer taking shots of the front façade of his house through strategic chinks in the hedge. He walked down the garden path to accost the man politely.

"Are you from Plum & Ottleys? It's not the *house* going on the market - only a couple of fields I want to part with, now that I'm getting a bit too old to keep them in order."

But since the man continued to snap away at Douglas as he approached, he realised he must not be from the Estate Agent after all. In confirmation Jim, the reporter, suddenly appeared in his gateway.

"We're from the Maplehurst Express, as a matter of fact. Just taking some snaps of the location. You might like to give us *your* side of the story, since we've just come from Damson Cottage...it's about that cat you executed by firing squad. The body reached Maplehurst this morning, and River Maintenance are none too chuffed."

Douglas' previously soaring spirits plunged earthwards. He had already berated himself for not engaging his brain in the aftermath of the shooting; he should have put a heavy stone in the sack to ensure it sank. Now he cursed himself for not suspecting a cat that canny would inevitably have a final card up its sleeve to trump him, though he still could not imagine how he had been fingered as the assassin. Had he been seen struggling in the dark with the sack? Perhaps his damn' neighbour had heard the gunshot after all, but chosen a more subtle method than rushing over and accosting him while still at the peak of her rage. *Much* smarter to wait, spin it to a newspaper, use propaganda to her advantage and get handsomely paid for her tragic story. What a fool he'd been!

Killing a cat was not a crime in the legal sense, of course, so no forensic team would come to match the bullets to his gun and arrest him. He *could* try to brazen it out. He wasn't facing prison - just a massacre by the newspapers, if Jim's self satisfied smirk was anything to go by. He decided a 'no comment' response would only make things worse so he attempted to bluff his way out of a tight corner.

"Cat? I've nothing to say about any *cat*. I shoot vermin, and of course I'll shoot at foxes if they come to raid my chickens."

He turned casually on his heel and strode off with what he hoped resembled dignity towards the house. In all the conflicting emotions of relief that the cat was no more, horror and embarrassment at being fingered as its killer, and now fear of an imminent mauling by the press, he still managed to feel a faint ripple of pride that his statement, which was completely off the cuff, contained no *outright* lie. For the creature he had killed was in all honesty not worthy of the name *cat*, plus he had deftly thrown in the cunning suggestion that he had shot what he *thought* was a fox, a plausible enough error in the darkness of night.

He assumed the story would only interest the local Maplehurst rag, but unfortunately Jim had more ambitious plans. He had a pal on one of the national tabloids with a sneaking penchant for stories which would land self-styled country squire types who still voted Tory in the mire, and this story had some interesting further ingredients.

"I've raked up some background ammo, Tony. It's perfect stuff! A lifetime of gunning things down, starting off in World War 2. A trail of dead pheasants, lots of shootin' and fishin', lives alone with a fierce guard dog, a snob, and before retirement Director of his own firm that made - wait for it - fishing gear: rods, hooks an' all the rest of the killing machinery!" Jim celebrated over the phone.

"What about the cat's owner? Nice, gentle, and maternal is she? No nasty skeletons there?"

"None what need see the light of day. 'Gentle' isn't the epithet that'd first spring to mind, but she does have two pre-teenage kids what'll tug at the emotions. And has just gone through the trauma of a divorce, so the cat's death could seem like a second bereavement."

"OK. Let's give it a go. Get some soppy pictures of the kids putting flowers on the cat's newly dug grave, and see if you can find any other villagers who'll dish more dirt on our Mr. Trigger-happy-Tomlinson."

Luckily for Douglas most of the villagers wanted no truck with nosey journalists and felt loyalty towards him, a resident of fifty years, rather than towards a newcomer who had so far haughtily avoided the local shops. Thus Jim's team were repeatedly disappointed by soppy stories of Douglas nursing his dying wife for two long years, and of his longstanding concern for his small and personal bird sanctuary where he would care for kestrels with broken wings, although of course there was no denial that he did fish in the river and sometimes shot pheasants with a group of other landowning gents.

The only eager detractor was Bella, a blousy, blubbery woman still smarting from the curt way in which he had brushed off her ardent, unrequited advances. Some years ago she had taken over the responsibility for church flowers after her own drunkard of a husband died leaving her virtually penniless, and therefore had the perfect excuse to hang around the new graves in the churchyard in the hope that a comfortably well-off widower might one day be so blinded by tears that he would find solace in her vast bosom. But she had made no headway whatsoever with Douglas.

> "He always hated cats *and* women," she declared, with what she fancied was a smile of irresistible charm, but eyes that glittered with malice. "He even preferred his bitch of a dog to his old wife, and he tried to have it off with *me* before she was properly dead. Then he rejected me *just like that* (she snapped three fat, sausagelike fingers) because of my darling little kitty-kitties - whom I wouldn't part with for anyone."

They wasted hours struggling in vain to capture a half-presentable portrait of her. Yet despite the flattering powers of super-subtle lighting she still looked so unappetising that no reader would consider his rejection cruel, but rather the exercise of supreme good sense.

The eventual story was spread across the centre pages, the headline blaring: TORY TOFF MURDERS MUM'S MUCH LOVED MOGGIE. There was a large, touching shot of the two kids erecting the headstone on the cat's grave; a wooden placard with the simple words *'Sheba we miss you'* scrawled in a wobbly, childish hand; another of the bereaved family group with the cat a distant white blob in the background; and a close up of Sheba herself, which despite lots of soft focus and sensitive airbrushing could not disguise the evil penetration of her unflinching stare. Very wisely, there was no picture of Bella. However her photos were not a complete waste of time, for they inspired the layout team to numerous lewd jokes - concerning the *real* reason he had shot Sheba up the arse.

The accompanying storyline was as fictitious as it was predictable. Only the short paragraph describing the finding of the cat's body had some vague basis in factual reality.

Needless to say Douglas did not buy a copy either of the tabloid or the Maplehurst Express, but he heard all about their coverage and his portrait as a serial cat-killer from concerned friends who called in to commiserate, plus local gossips who phoned up principally to gloat. He had a spate of hate mail from cat lovers up and down the country and someone painted *Effing Murderer!* in thick red paint across the side of his car when he rashly parked it in the village to replenish his stock of food. But he found that if he stayed indoors, or went out only for dawn or twilight walks on his own land, he was reasonably safe from attack.

From time to time provocative objects (chunks of raw meat, sometimes a flea-ridden hedgehog flattened by a passing car or some other road-kill corpse) would be tossed over the hedge bordering the lane, accompanied by wild, bloodthirsty hunting cries or some seriously slanderous chanting. Yet this kind of thing was chiefly confined to weekends, when tourists came from afar to view the infamous murder scene, or pilgrims who took their love of cats to sacred extremes had the time to travel.

Jim remained his most steadfast persecutor, launching an all out campaign to get his gun license revoked, on the grounds that someone who could not distinguish between a cat's and a fox's rear end at forty paces in the dark had failing eyesight and should not be allowed to handle a gun. Perhaps a control experiment was conducted, with a cross-section of the far sighted community put to the test, all of whom failed; - whatever yardstick was applied it must have exonerated Douglas of blame, for no-one came to confiscate his gun despite Jim's relentless pressure. In truth, Douglas would not have minded too much if they had since he had little use for it now that his pheasant shooting buddies no longer invited him to join them, fearing he would bring a veritable army of angry protesters in his wake.

It was roughly two months after the fateful shooting of Sheba when he finally crossed paths with his neighbour from Damson Cottage. The hate mob visits had died to almost nothing by then, so he had dared to risk a brisk walk down the lane to where he could enter the spinney - and there she was, jogging on the spot beside a holly bush, and it looked as if she were actually waiting for him. He thought of turning back but that seemed pathetic and cowardly, so he carried on looking steadfastly ahead, hoping he could pass her without making eye contact. He had just about made it when he heard her voice, uncharacteristically subdued, say:

"Could I have a word, Mr Tomlinson?"

25

"When have I ever been in a position to stop *you* talking?" He spoke quietly, but there was a world of bitterness behind his words.

"I owe you an apology. So I'm trying to say sorry."

He stared at her incredulously. She looked rather pale and tremulous - unless this was her real self beneath the make-up, and he therefore fleetingly wondered if her alimony might have been cut off by a vengeful ex-husband jealous, no doubt, of her excessive tabloid payout bonanza. Or perhaps the very same tabloid was now trying to recoup its expenses by exposing some of *her* dirty secrets.

"You were right about that cat, you know. I just couldn't see it at the time, but it was malicious through and through. We're only just returning to normal ourselves, me and the kids - I guess it had us all in thrall. I bought a young tabby kitten the other day and it's *so* incredibly cute. That's what finally made me realise."

Douglas remained silent, digesting the news. He had been through hell and high floodwater from his inability to cope with both feline predators: cat *and* woman. He had been wrong to rid the world of the cat, he had long been able to admit that to himself, so the last thing he now wanted was to be wrong in how he dealt with her. Her apparent vulnerability appealed to some nearly dormant instinct of sympathy and protection, but swinging him violently the other way was a fury that she had taunted and provoked him to the extent she had, until he had gone against his own normally tolerant nature and then become such a very public scapegoat as a result. It was as if one hand ached to put a comforting arm around her; while the other itched to shake her so roughly that all the false notions flew out of her head. In the end, typical of his age, gender and upbringing, he chose a compromise.

"I was right about the cat," he admitted wryly, "but wrong in the way I dealt with it. Instead of shooting it while its back was turned, I should have fought it fairly face to face, using teeth and claws."

She looked up at him with mournful, humbled eyes, but Douglas could see that beyond the stain of sadness lurked the glimmer of resurgeant humour and mischief.

"Well, that way you'd have lost for certain," she assured him. But without any of the spite or annoying superiority of earlier times.

When in Rome…

Florence in the spring time - what a lucky girl! Except that she had gone there to learn Italian and to speak it fluently, meaningfully, even poetically; not simply ask the way to a train station with the correct inflexion and an accent that did not instantly declare her Englishness.

But owing to the nervous disposition of her elderly parents, who were deeply alarmed by the wolfish reputation of Italian males with their salacious appetite for pale young female flesh from northerly climes, her whole Italian adventure was stifled from the start. After an unnerving foretaste of dozens of pink, salivating tongues and eyes that undressed on one of those 'motoring' holidays through Italy when Lauren was only fourteen and still mercifully under-developed, they knew that now she was eighteen it could only be worse. They therefore arranged for her to stay safely 'supervised' (or so the brochure implied) at Signora Umberti's, and from there attend daily classes run by the staid and sensible British Council, to strictly limit her hours of dangerous exposure.

There was surely a learning experience in it somewhere, Lauren mused, but whatever got learnt it was *not* Italian. Signora Umberti was a widow who smiled charmingly, sighed eloquently, but rarely uttered a word. Doubtless she had once had lots to say to her husband before he died, and certainly she could compete volubly with her neighbour whenever they argued over the rubbish, and precisely whose fault it was that a scavenger dog had strewn it across the courtyard. But because none of her six paying guests could speak more than a feeble, halting Italian she was rendered speechless; and they, to avoid the awkwardness of silent meal times, resorted to speaking English amongst themselves.

It was not what the brochure had promised. *'All our students enjoy the 'total immersion' method, living and breathing Italian as part of a genuine Italian family with constant exposure to the Italian language.'*

Well, they must never have checked out Signora Umberti's, - since when was a widow living alone a 'family'? And how was Italian likely to be the dominant language when only one out of seven could speak it?

After the first day Signora Umberti studiously avoided them, especially at meal times. She delivered the steaming dishes, flashed a radiant smile, then hurried off to the comfort of her little sitting room with its tiny television, which to her was the real world where people spoke properly in Italian.

Lauren surveyed her fellow diners with a certain dismay. She could honestly sympathise with Signora Umberti - these people were heavy-going conversationalists even in their own tongue. All were more than double her age; while Letitia, the eldest, was nudging ninety. She in fact spoke volumes for the success of the British Council's teaching methods, having come on these courses faithfully every spring for thirty five years - yet *still* unable to string one coherent sentence together. Mind you, both her short and middle term memories were unreliable. All she had a firm handle on were a few select happenings when she was Lauren's age (which she never tired of retelling Lauren), so it was perhaps unfair on the British Council to consider her a typical student.

Had Lauren not met an American Fine Arts graduate on a Fulbright scholarship she would be packing for home by now, in the sixth and final week of the course, yet still useless at Italian apart from being able to snap, *"Sta zita, non ti amo!"* at a lone wolf who regularly sniffed out her tracks however imaginatively she varied her route to classes. Merle (the American girl) kindly offered her a mattress on the floor of her studio flat so she could stay on to find an au pairing job, and thus get to live with an authentic Italian family and hopefully learn some Italian.

She first met Merle at the same rubbish bin where Signora Umberti had tackled her irate neighbour. Merle assembled huge collages, and her favourite raw material was egg shells which, although organic, apparently lasted for ever. This was crucially important, she told Lauren, because an artist friend of hers had been sued when his artwork fell apart after four years owing to using some flimsy, impermanent material. The poor guy had to pay back more than he charged for it in the first place, so as to compensate for its failure to price inflate! *She* did not want any similar disasters ruining her tenuous career. So every day she trawled through a different street's rubbish to collect enough egg shells, and sometimes she went to a wasteland behind the Pirelli garage to strip live snails from the stalks of tall anaemic weeds.

It was only after Lauren had moved in with her that she realised just how vile a process it was to prise those snails out of their shells *without* damaging them (the shells that is, for the snails were of course brutally massacred).

She had not explained to Lauren that she was a lesbian, so it was fortunate that she already had a lesbian friend to share her bed with. In fact, as Lauren lay on her mattress on the kitchen floor on her first night of freedom listening to their agitations in the bedroom, she celebrated her lucky escape. She could have been resisting being molested right now, and although she knew it was a false parallel, shadowy images of wolves, grandmamas and a solitary little red riding hood wandered uneasily through her mind.

In the morning they ate their obligatory breakfast of boiled eggs, and in between mouthfuls Florentina, Merle's partner, a black American also on a scholarship (a different one) told her that art and eggs had had a long, shared history. The Renaissance painters she had to study always mixed dollops of egg white into their colours for greater lustre and a more malleable texture. After dutifully rinsing out the egg shells they walked to the University to pin up a notice offering Lauren as an au pair.

It had surprisingly prompt results. The following day Merle's phone moaned and vibrated (ringing had a detrimental effect on your ovaries, apparently) and a man's voice with a thick purr invited her to meet him at his hotel. She had the wit to remember to check that he genuinely had children (seemingly so, for he was ready with names - although less certain of their ages), and she dexterously chose the earlier hour of six rather than the dangerously late one of eleven, they being the limited choices he offered.

He looked very much what he was; a semi-famous singer somewhat beyond his prime, a night club crooner of the old fashioned mould who still fancied himself - but was beginning to worry that others might not. His name was Bruno Valentino, and it suited him for some reason she could not quite put her finger on.

He was not bothered by what Lauren had done or could do, and cared not a jot for her academic certificates. All he wanted to know was whether she had a 'wealthy accent' (*maybe* she did, she told him, since she came from near Tunbridge Wells), and that her looks would mesh favourably with his public image.

Satisfied on both counts he pulled out a black leather wallet embossed with his name and withdrew a fistful of crisp new notes, moistening his lips with his tongue and passing a critical eye over Lauren's seated figure as he did so.

She left with the train fare from Florence to Viareggio plus a little extra for the buffet and a taxi to the house, and instructions to arrive around midday the following Saturday. It fell somewhere short of the *perfect* situation because she had wanted to look after lovable little kids with piping voices and shining eyes, whereas these two were teenagers, a boy and a girl. But at least it was a job, and it gave her some solid information to tell her parents and assuage their worries.

That night she went to celebrate her luck with Merle and Florentina at a local trattoria. They expansively ordered T-bone steak with wild porcini mushrooms, for Merle had tried this ruse before - cunningly persuading the waiter to wrap up the uneaten half of her steak 'for her dog'. She then eked out the meal for three more suppers, with soup from the bone on the fourth, calculating that it was almost more economical than eating at home. This careful economy was a necessity because Fulbright scholarships were not as generous as they sounded, and despite her constant sifting through rubbish she still had to invest in dozens of eggs every week. On this occasion, what with the sumptuous haul of unchewed flesh on three T-bones and Lauren about to leave anyway, so no longer part of the equation, she was anticipating a whole week of suppers for two. Which she jubilantly readjusted to a fortnight when she saw the generously bulging bag their waiter brought them.

"Courtesy of the chef," he said with a grin and a wink, "we've added more bones - I know what appetites those wolf hounds have!"

When they got home and eagerly upended the bag, however, it was certainly full of bones - but none that gave any sustenance. They had precious little flesh *or* marrow, in fact if it were not for the inclusion an odd mangetout and occasional bruised spinach leaf one would never suspect they had emerged from a restaurant, or not recently. They reminded Lauren of the rattling, greyish collection that had gingerly been passed around the class for a 'hands on' anatomy lesson back at school. Florentina even fell to wondering darkly whether they might not be of human rather than bovine origin. And, to add insult to injury, the three succulent T-bones they had so abstemiously left with huge chunks of meat on were conspicuously missing!

"Bastards!" Merle raged, "Lesbophobic bloody bastards! I'd like to buy an effing wolf hound now and train it to kill 'em!"

"Well, we did try to play a trick on them," Lauren pointed out, "since there *is* no wolf hound. I only wish I'd finished my steak now," she added wistfully.

Florentina sniffed the bones suspiciously, "Hmm, lesbophobic maybe - but at least they're not racist. In my home town they'd have doused them in petrol or poison, but these seem squeaky clean."

Lauren scurried to the bathroom, for the pile of bones suddenly had an unsettling digestive effect. Somewhat shakily she surveyed the container that had once housed body butter (or so its label proclaimed) but now hosted Merle's impressive collection of finger and toenail clippings, which apparently had similar properties to egg and snail shells and were therefore safe to use on collages. The decisive factor, Merle had explained, was not that they should truly last for *ever* but more precisely the full duration of the artist's life, or certainly *this artist's* life, because as Merle planned never to have a family her non-existent progeny could never be sued. Lauren in her faintly queasy state felt thankful that Merle at least had her penchant for these hard, dry, brittle things that barely smelt at all. She was not sure she could have kept any food down if Merle had been a pickler and stewer, an always-dunking-things-in-formaldehyde type of artist like Damian Hirst.

It was while her mind speculated idly with elements that decay and elements which do not that an idea suddenly came to her.

"Why not use the bones in a collage, Merle? They'd last *your* lifetime - they'd probably survive a few thousand years!"

Merle stared at her, "Je-esus, fuck me for a fool!" and a low whistle rattled her lips, "Bone Art - sounds kinda snazzy…I dunno why *I* didn't think of it myself! If I play my cards right I could have a whole lousy chain of restaurants offloading their redundant bones onto me! I'll lease a workshop, hire disciples - just like those jammy Renaissance geniuses Florentina worships."

"Steady on," warned Florentina, but whether from sheer good sense or advance jealousy of Merle's future circus of apprentices Lauren could not be sure.

Lauren felt almost tearful over her goodbyes at the train station. She would miss her mattress on the floor in their company, and she might never ever get to meet such an interesting lesbian-cross-cultural couple again. They busily gave her plenty of last minute advice.

"Remember - befriend the wife, that's the way to au pairing success. And keep that husband's greedy paws off you," Florentina warned.

"If you bother to stay in touch I might send you royalties from my sales of bone work," Merle disliked goodbyes and spoke grumpily.

"You're too much like egg white, Lauren. Keep your lustre - that's beautiful; but don't be so darn' malleable. It'll do you *no* favours."

Lauren smiled and waved, and wiped a tear from her eye as the train slowly rumbled out of the station.

Lauren's vision of the Mediterranean was of flaming flowers, whispering pines and smooth grey-speckled cliffs tumbling into a deep blue sea fading to turquoise, for that 'motoring' holiday aged fourteen had taken her to the more picturesque parts of the Riviera and then south to the Gulf of Salerno. Her disappointment was therefore acute when the land flattened drably after the train left the Arno valley at Pisa and they travelled through a modern, densely built wasteland of ugliness to the so-called resort (presumably a last one) of Viareggio. It was obvious now that the reason the Tower of Pisa had originally begun to lean was simply because all the people of medieval times who climbed up it stood only on the landward side to look admiringly at the folds of Tuscan hills, and no-one braved the hideous view of Viareggian mudflats to act as a stabilising counterweight.

Lauren showed the taxi driver the Valentino address and sat despondently on the backseat, trying desperately to rekindle the fires of her optimism. I came to learn Italian, she reminded herself, not for the beauty of the view.

But learning Italian was the opposite of what Signora Valentino had in mind.

"We want them speaking perfect English," she announced, her voice so sharp it could have sliced through prosciutto, "not to waste their summer mooching about like slobs. You'll speak always and only in English, *capisci?*"

"Capisco," Lauren murmured, a little taken aback by the look of pure hatred La Signora cast her way.

As she struggled up the stairs with her heavy suitcase that now felt infinitely heavier, she overheard a sudden volley of anger and accusations from the living room, where La Signora had immediately run to phone her husband and berate him for his outlandish choice of au pair.

"She's a mere *bambina*. I know why you chose her, *cretino ripulsivo*! We agreed on an English governess of forty who can control the fucking kids, so you pick a mere schoolgirl for her golden hair and apple breasts to drool at - *che disgrazia!*"

But learning English was nowhere on the kids' agenda. Curiosity brought them knocking at Lauren's door immediately. Luigi was fourteen, exactly Lauren's height and with already the dark shadowing of a moustache on his upper lip; Miranda was thirteen, short and stumpy like her parents, and she never ceased tossing her lovely, luxurious mane of auburn hair. Both were delighted that Lauren looked so young and such an easy pushover.

"Hey, let's get things straight from *il principio*. *Uno*, our parents are the pits. *Due, w*e won't be learning English. *Tre,* it's holiday time, when all our friends hang out; so, you can join in, have fun. But try any English on us and you can go straight *all' diabolo!*"

"Capisco benissimo," Lauren replied. She understood him perfectly because her Italian had improved beyond recognition in the mere five days since leaving Signora Umberti's, and perhaps, under Luigi's strict conditions, it might carry on improving after all.

Signora Valentino remained in her boudoir for the next first twenty four hours, but certainly not incommunicado for her powerful voice penetrated the walls, barking orders or baying with alternate laughter or rage into her mobile phone. The maid meanwhile slipped discreetly in and out bearing trays of fat-free food with jugs of iced lemonade and, on alternate visits, a flask of black coffee and a bumper sized bottle of aspirin.

Lauren sauntered around the affluent sector of beachfront villas with the kids, wondering if this listless, indolent existence was what Luigi meant by 'having fun'. It was apparently too hot to play tennis, too cold to go swimming, too late for beach volleyball, too early to catch a movie, and too boring to see his friends.

Miranda moaned as she tried to keep up with his long-legged, loping pace, for she had developed a blister from her mother's borrowed high heels and Luigi was purposefully trying to give her the slip.

"She's in our way. She's just too young," he whispered, giving Lauren a conspiratorial wink with eyes that already seemed adept at undressing.

La Signora returned to circulation the following evening. Dramatic changes had taken place. Her hair was two inches shorter, had switched from black to deep burgundy with champagne highlights and, instead of nuzzling her collar affectionately, now stood on end as if alarmed by something vindictive the collar had said. She had lost weight, gained height (due to the hair), swapped brown eyes for green, and had a lovely mousse-induced tan. The only element of continuity was that she still looked at Lauren through narrowed, hostile eyes.

"So, how is their English coming along?"

"*Cosi cosi*," Lauren admitted truthfully, "they're not very keen."

"Then you must *make* them keen."

Family supper was joyless. Mama's dieting was patently torture. She grimaced, chewed in slow motion and sighed like the wind in the poplar trees that lined their driveway; then, the calorie limit reached, thrust her plate away with an aggressive clang. Thereafter she chatted in staccato bursts into her mobile, staring venomously at Lauren during the obligatory intervals of listening to her phone companion. Luigi meanwhile ate like a horse and snorted like one too, whilst Miranda sniffed and picked at her food, staring mournfully at the centrepiece bowl of wilting lilies.

And all the time Lauren kept up the charade of teaching English, intoning slowly, sweetly, clearly - and of course utterly pointlessly.

"Please pass the water."

"Huh."

"Would you like some more bread?"

"Nuh."

"This cheese is delicious."

Silence.

"Thank you, I have eaten enough."

Silence.

"How long have you lived in Viareggio?"

Silence.

"In England we like to eat Italian food. It's even better than French cuisine."

"A *French* word!" La Signora's hand whipped across the mouthpiece of her mobile faster than an executioner's axe, "How DARE you! You know the rules - *solo Inglese!*"

"I'm so sorry."

"Che dici?"

"Mi scusi, per piacere."

It was never destined to last. Lauren's downfall was inevitable, and - she was prepared to admit - entirely her own fault. She had tried and tried to coax English words from their lips at meal times, or at least kindle the faintest light of comprehension in their eyes when she spoke to them, but Miranda silently sulked while Luigi's grunts became daily more erotically suggestive.

On the day of debacle a hot, sweaty Sirocco wind blew straight from the blistering south creating an eerie, otherworldly light. It sent La Signora's blood pressure soaring dangerously. Her moodometre needle swivelled round beyond anger, past fury, and all the way to dementia itself. The kids knew from past experience to keep well out of her way, and as the sultry wind attracted no-one outside they retired downstairs to their subterranean den in the bowels of the house where computers, game consoles, flat-screen TVs and music systems had been installed for their entertainment. Luigi rummaged through his floor to ceiling stack of CDs for something to impress Lauren.

"D'you want to be a singer, like your dad?" she asked him.

"I want to be *nothing* like him. *Che cretino!* How can anyone sing like that these days? Man, he's fifty years outta' date!"

"OK. So what *do* you want to be?"

"A rapper. I'm bloody good at that. Hey - I know what you could do, and it's *kind of* like teaching me English. We could listen to some American rappers I like, and you could translate them into Italian."

"OK." Lauren by this time would have jumped at anything that actually enthused either of them, and by this time she had honestly lost hope that anything on this earth could conceivably enthuse Miranda.

So, during several hours of repeat listening she carefully transcribed the 'lyrics' of three of his favourite numbers, laboriously translating them into Italian with the help of a dictionary and Luigi himself - who was so wired up he was a changed character. He whirled around the room like a matador all the while assembling his gear, endlessly readjusting the height of his microphone stand and fighting the whines of feedback, changing his mind back and forth over which backing track he preferred - as if he were launching his solo career in one massive public performance.

"Keep the volume down," she advised nervously, "the words are kind of dirty."

"The dirtier the better!" and he laughed with wild abandon while thrusting out his loins.

He should have said the *louder* the better. Both she and Miranda flinched and shuddered as if administered a powerful electric shock, then smothered their ears against the explosion of decibels which reverberated through the room. This thunderous wall of sound shivered the window panes, warped the ceiling and tinkled the cymbals of the drum kit Bruno had recently bought him - just in case, one miraculous day, Luigi should relent hostilities, learn humility and agree to become his drummer.

When Lauren by slow degrees removed her fingers from her eardrums she could hear that Luigi genuinely knew how to rap. He had an unusual voice that combined elements of papa's honied crooning and mama's stentorian bark, plus punctuations of his own which reminded her of the erotic grunting he had been so assiduously practising at mealtimes. She urgently crawled across the floor to turn down his volume, but sadly too late - the opening salvo of ear shattering sound had shaken the house to its very foundations, tossed mama out of bed, rattled her make-up bottles and, worst of all, revived the ferocity of her skull-splitting migraine.

Miranda was the first to notice her mother standing in the doorway, her compact body wrapped in a silk dressing gown with leopardskin markings and her burgundy hair entirely vertical - as if voltage as surcharged as Luigi's decibels had zipped through it. With an angry jab from a purple painted fingernail she tripped the electrical supply to the basement, darkness swamped them and Luigi's voice faded on a particularly sexually surcharged swearword. In the twilit confusion that followed, her senses dazed by the sizzling sounds of complaint from her ears, Lauren heard with trepidation Miranda's whimpers and some unidentified snorts of fury from a shape in the doorway. She guessed from the sinking feeling in her stomach that it must be La Signora.

With a sharp 'click' artificial light once more flooded the room. Not the subdued night club effect Luigi had contrived but the dazzling white beams of cheap striplighting which harshly illuminated every hidden niche. In strode La Signora to snatch the sheaf of lyrics from Luigi's grasp, and all three quaked in fear as her red rimmed eyes perused them. She had scarcely got through the first 'verse' before ripping them to shreds, and the fragments were still floating gently to the floor like snowflakes when she swung round to impale Lauren with green-red eyes of loathing.

"You are paid to teach them Queen's English, not pornographic filth!" she hissed. "You're *out of here* girl!"

Luigi coughed in consternation, Miranda continued to whimper and La Signora indulged in her own coughing fit to allow some of her anger to convert to steam. During this uneasy interval Lauren silently berated herself, acknowledging that the lyrics were unwisely provocative, especially in their references to mothers and what they deserved done to them; yet she praised her tiny iota of caution that had - at least - toned down (and mercifully once even omitted) the very vilest epithets and obscenest references to those private places of female anatomy.

How dismally had she failed to follow Florentina's advice: 'Befriend the wife'!

La Signora, recovered from a bout of hyperventilation following the coughing, came menacingly close to eyeball her.

"Out of here girl!" she shrieked again, as if it were a chorus to conclude Luigi's song. "You've five minutes to decide where. I'll buy you a ticket to anywhere in Italy - forget France or England. I'll pay four days' wages plus ticket, no more. Pack your bag *prontissimo.*"

Lauren, dazed as she was, performed some quick thinking. She could return to Florence and pin up another notice, or she could try for Turin which was closest to the border, and from there phone her parents for the journey money home, but either choice struck her as an admission of abject failure. Venice attracted her with the romance of gondolas, misty canals, arched bridges and Canaletto brought to life, but her confidence had sunk so low she did not want to go somewhere that was sinking itself. Naples beckoned with its beautiful coastal inlets around Positano and the drama of Mount Vesuvius, but with her current run of luck she would only reactivate the volcano…

"Roma," she said, the faintest gleam of defiance fighting the tears of rejection and the wounded look she was determined La Signora should not see.

She was then brutally swept away by a taxi without the chance to say goodbye to either of the children.

The train rumbled sluggishly south into the teeth of Sirocco, the air itself smelling of bad breath and stagnation. Lauren tried to keep her spirits up, but it was difficult to ignore the obvious evidence that this Italian venture of hers was doomed. Her sojourn at Signora Umberti's had taught her that only people with nothing happening in their lives chose language courses in Italy. *Why* had she wanted to learn Italian? Beset by the hot stale air of the railway carriage, she had bewilderingly forgotten her motive.

She had chosen the wrong au pairing job, that much was certain. *And* made serious mistakes whilst there. The question that hung over her now, as she trundled south in severe discomfort (La Signora had bought the cheapest possible ticket to Rome on the slowest train in Italy), was whether she had stupidly compounded her problems by going the wrong way instead of heading safely homewards. Her four days' pay jingled plaintively in her pocket; barely enough to purchase a T-bone steak in the trattoria in Florence, and definitely not enough for ice cream afterwards. Perhaps, if she slept on the streets and lived off bread and water, she might just about survive another week.

E periculoso sporgiarsi advised a grimy, greasy notice above the window, but in this cattle train there was not even the opportunity to kill yourself by leaning out and losing your head, for the window was jammed firmly and irrevocably shut.

"They say hell's hotter and more depressing," her co-sufferer in the carriage opined after he had painfully pulled the muscles in his back trying to open the window, "but I doubt it."

The train not only stopped at every conceivable station en route, it also stopped for no apparent reason in between them.

Why had she not swallowed her pride and returned to Florence, to become a disciple of Merle's and glue bones? Or at least volunteered to collect them like a good little rag and bone girl, so those with greater skills could do the glueing? The journey from Florence to Viareggio had taken just over an hour. She would be laughing with Merle and Florentina about her Valentino mistake by now had she made that choice, but as it was, three and a half sweaty hours later, they had limped to somewhere parallel with Elba, the island where Napoleon was imprisoned all those many years ago. *Able was I ere I saw Elba* she muttered, recalling the abstruse palindrome from a classroom competition and stifling the sob of realisation that she had not proved herself 'able' at all!

After eight long hours the train at last staggered into Rome and Lauren made a feeble effort to freshen up. She wiped the worst smears of grime from her face with the cleanest section of her T-shirt moistened with sweat from her forehead, for the toilet facilities on the train, such as they were (or truthfully were not) did not extend to taps or running water. Then she dragged her suitcase to a bench outside the station and sat there, wondering listlessly what to do. The Sirocco had been replaced by a feebler but still sickly breeze, and it was already early evening. She eyed her bulky suitcase morosely, wishing it would magically transform into a lightweight backpack more suitable for her new rootless, penniless state. It was far too heavy - yet too small to sleep in, and too dangerous as well, because its wheels would make her perilously easy to abduct.

Across the piazza a pink neon sign flashed on and off. Invest your money in the *sigurezza della Banca d'Italia*, it kept advising. *What money?* Lauren thought balefully - then suddenly the name stirred her memory. *Of course!* During last year's A level studies at the tutorial college she had attended in

Oxford (her school had unfairly refused her admittance into the sixth form, due to an incident that faintly foreshadowed the one that just got her fired from the Valentinos) she had had a relationship with an Italian postgraduate student called Paolo. It was during the summer term, poorly timed in the chaotic midst of her exams. He was doing a Masters degree in economics funded by this very same Banca d'Italia, so he would surely have to be working there right now to honour the funding.

Except that honour and he had some rather strange arrangements that were coming back to her now, as her memory sharpened into focus. He had enjoyed a very lucrative sideline writing Masters' dissertations for numerous employees of this very same bank, ones who were becalmed midway up the hierarchy of command, unable to progress without an advanced degree.

"But isn't that cheating?" she had asked in her seventeen year old innocence.

He was perplexed by such an interpretation. "No, no. Not in Italy. Such a thing is absolutely normal. For us exams and theses are a challenge to succeed by whatever means; he who cheats cleverly is a clever person, and thus deserves to succeed. Examiners are like policemen for us - authority figures we *must* get the better of."

"Oh," was all she said then.

"Posso parlare con Paolo Moravia?" she said now, squeezed into a tiny booth alongside her suitcase, having dialled the number of the Bank's head office that was fitfully illuminated in wild pink neon across the piazza.

"Lauren - what a surprise!" he either exulted or regretted, she could not tell in her stupefied state of exhaustion. "Where are you, amore?"

"In Rome. Outside the main station."

"Dio mio - I'll come immediately!"

He had been neither the very first nor the only one to share a sexual encounter with whilst she was in Oxford (unknown to her parents, of course), but she had to admit he had been the most appetizing. She had recklessly, foolishly abandoned her virginity to a fresh faced fresher, and in doing so disappointingly discovered that below his face all his freshness disappeared. Instead there was an angry rash of acne across his whole torso, while some kind of grey, virulent mould sprouted between his toes, and the curdled smell of his sheets made her queasy - but she was much too polite to let him know. Her second affair was just as woefully disappointing and physically distasteful, so that Paolo had been a blessed relief. Not only was he equally as attractive naked as clothed, but he even knew how to make love *properly*!

In Oxford he always wore jeans and a sweater (England was so cold and damp he insisted, even in the height of summer) and looked like a student. But now he arrived snappily dressed in an elegant summer suit with tie and cufflinks and all the paraphernalia of success Italian style, which only made her feel dirtier than ever. He then drove with reckless abandon, swerving round corners and other cars and swooping into the gaps in the traffic with the skill of a born queue barger, and since he always stopped a millimetre short of the car in front whilst looking not ahead but at her, she guessed he had some seventh sense of spatial awareness that prevented accidents.

After the slow, chugging, linear movement of the train his driving made her stomach churn and her head spin, especially the sudden dives down dark narrow alleyways that were apparently brilliant short cuts. Had he been a kidnapper taking her to his secret lair he could not have chosen a more mind-boggling route, without any need for a blindfold. Her first impression of Rome was thus of a confused, subterranean rabbit warren of criss-crossing pedestrian alleyways, with occasional magnificent tall buildings rising up above the gloom into a world of golden sunlit architectural beauty.

"There's the Colosseum!" he gesticulated left as they did a slewing wheel spin round a sharp bend and ran over a plump rat in the act of stealing a crimson hunk of salami. But by the time she looked back the Colosseum had vanished.

At last they stopped in a cobbled alleyway which in London would be called a Mews, and Paolo suddenly disappeared like the white rabbit into a tangle of wisteria. Moments later his face thrust through the dangling clumps of soft blue flowers high above her, looking anxiously down.

"Aren't you coming in?"

Groping amongst the platted trunks and branches that were so well established they must be centuries old, she eventually found an open doorway and climbed the stairs to what felt like a tree house. It seemed so firmly gripped in the stranglehold of wisteria branches that it would surely collapse if a tidy minded gardener decided to prune.

"It's like Oxford but with sunshine, don't you think?"

"It's very beautiful," she agreed, "how *did* you find it?"

"Someone owed me a favour," he said enigmatically, "but I must move in three days, very, very sadly."

"Why?"

"Oh - later, it's such a long story. First you must tell me all about yourself. Oh, Lauren, so beautiful *amore*, now that you are eighteen!"

"You said exactly that when I was seventeen."

"Yes, yes. But it's much, much more true now."

She had an uneasy feeling they had parted company last year on a bad note, some quarrel connected with his dishonesty or insincerity, but she could no longer remember the essence of it, and right now she badly needed a shower to wash away the effect of a long hot train journey and a remorseless Sirocco. Afterwards he cooked them supper, and as they ate she told him all about her experiences with the Valentino family.

"Such people - I don't mean to be a snob *amore* - but they are *brutto*, no breeding, no education, no imagination, *niente*. You absolutely must avoid those types - they will never treat you properly. Oh Lauren, *tesoro mio*, in Rome you will be sure to find the right family!"

"How?"

"*Facilissimo!* Tomorrow we will pin up notices in the *right* places, where only people of genuine intelligence and good breeding will see them."

He became exuberantly expansive, plying her with reassurances like presents at Christmastime. He would in future be her guardian angel, gallantly protecting her from all the vulgar, ogling husbands and their vindictive, jealous wives; showing her in the meantime the matchless grace and everlasting beauty that was Rome, with all its magnificent history that put Oxford so miserably, pathetically to shame. With his careful, thoughtful guidance she would learn that Italians could be truly honourable and, of course, the most fascinating men in the world! That night she would receive the first lesson; a refresher course as it were - for the elementary stages had all of course been gone through in Oxford; the knowledge to be imparted being the indisputable fact that Italian men are the very best lovers in the world. In Oxford such lessons had been curtailed by her curfew hour, but here in Rome he was at her disposal all night long.

"OK," he said eventually over breakfast next morning, which was a tall mug of caffe con latte and an energy renewing slice of ripe, juicy melon. "Tell me what was less than *perfezione*, and I promise that tonight I will make it *even* better."

"If you make me the judge or examiner, you'll only be tempted to cheat."

"Oh Lauren - so young and yet so very cunning, how I love you!"

"I guess," she said, her hands gingerly exploring the tender areas on her cheeks and jawline, "you *could* try shaving beforehand. That way you wouldn't nearly skin me alive. You wanted my opinion," she reminded him, in case he took offence.

"Va bene," he agreed, looking not offended but remarkably pleased, "such a quick beard is a sure sign of my awesome virility."

They wrote two notices advertising Lauren as an au pair. One they pinned up in the central noticeboard in the UN Headquarters for Food and Agriculture, which they did together, and the second Paolo promised to place in the Banca d'Italia, but on no account should she go there with him, or try to visit him there.

"Why?" she asked, curious, since he had seemed so proud to be with her up until then. "Are you ashamed of me?"

He laughed loudly. "Oh-ho, you are so funny - of course I'm not! It's just I'm going to be late for work this morning. Yesterday I left running when you phoned me, if I can't concentrate all through today for daydreaming of you, and I'm late *again* tomorrow...why, if they see you, they'll *know* my heart's no longer in my work!"

So Lauren wandered around Rome on foot, alone. Whereas Florence was provincial she found Rome very much the capital city - and very consciously so. It was more Baroque less Renaissance, more crowded, more political, more associated with the ancient times of Empires and had far more serious deprivation in its slum areas. Wrapped around the Colosseum she found a section of extreme poverty where kids went barefoot and mothers begged in doorways, and she guessed both the rat that Paolo ran over yesterday - plus the salami it had stolen - would have immediately been scooped up for somebody's supper.

Later on she threw a coin in the Trevi fountain and wished for a kind family to answer her advert. She also made herself a personal promise that if she had not found work within three days she would give up, phone her parents and dejectedly go home. She would probably have given herself a little more time if she had been more independent, but Paolo seemed particularly keen on the three day cut-off point since it coincided so neatly with his moving out of the Mews cottage.

In the evening she met Paolo in the shadow of a prearranged doorway, and he drove her wildly all over the city, visiting beautiful Boromini churches and Bernini monuments and praising the art and artistry of past Italian men of genius. Then, to temper his kilos of boastfulness over Italy's glorious history with a gramme of truth about its lesser moments he took her on a 'Mussolini' tour. Together they jeered at Mussolini's desolate modern sector with its laughably pompous triumphal arch aping the old Roman gateway, and they scoffed at the arrogance of his silly balcony on the impressive palazzo in the centre of Rome from which he spoke eloquent deceptions to the ignorant masses.

"You said you were a communist," she reminded him, "in Oxford, when we saw that Pasolini film. Are you still?"

"I was a student then," he reminded her with a nervous laugh, "students are *always* communist - until they start to earn too much."

Later on that night he strove to convince her that, even if he might have lost his political ideology, he had not lost his romantic idealism, and she of all women in the world was his romantic ideal. Apparently muses were the invention of the Italian man, as was love itself - and candlelight, and the vocabulary and artistry of making love.

"'If you have to keep saying it then it ain't true' - that's a bit of Anglo-Saxon commonsense for you," Lauren told him, after she felt so stuffed with hyperbole and compliments she feared she might burst. "Remember us English are the masters of understatement. Just like you Italians are the masters, it seems, of everything else."

On their third and final night Paolo lit many candles and toasted the sadness of her imminent departure in finest wine. She was about to steel herself to phone her parents and admit defeat when the phone suddenly rang of its own accord. Paolo scurried urgently to pick it up. She could not hear the voice on the other end but she watched the rapidly changing emotions play across his face; curiosity, puzzlement, surprise, shock and finally something strangely close to fear. She had privately suspected that his enforced move from this house, which he had repeatedly refused to worry her about, was actually due to his having been caught out in some sharp practice too sharp even for Italian standards, so she was truly taken aback when he handed her the phone:

"It's for you."

More surprises were in store. On the other end of the line was Signora Martinelli, with a voice that was warm and relaxed, offering her an au pairing job for the summer holidays looking after her two little daughters aged four and six, and wanting to see her tomorrow morning to talk things through. That was her first - and best - surprise.

The unexpected surprise was the effect it had on Paolo. He looked visibly shaken, and the glass of wine he downed in one gulp had the mark of desperation rather than celebration.

"Aren't you pleased I've got a job?" she asked, deeply puzzled by his strange reaction, "or did you make some *crazy* bet that I wouldn't, and you're now about to go bankrupt?"

He sat down, pale as death, "No, no. There was no bet. It's not that, no, no."

"Then what *is* it? Are you feeling ill?"

"Yes, ill," he said, staring fixedly at the floor. "Lauren I…I have to tell you …something."

But he seemed quite unable to continue.

"You've been caught cheating? The police are after you? Don't worry, you'll slip out of it, that's just one of the very minor things Italian men are best at!"

But he shook his head, stood up, then sat abruptly down again. At last he took a deep breath and spoke hoarsely. "Lauren - I can't…see you anymore, not at all, tesoro."

"You're being *blackmailed,* is that it? Or, something *more* dangerous…?"

Again he shook his head. "No, no. I'm…I'm about to be formally engaged to someone, my *fidenzata,* and after eight weeks of engagement we will be married. All the invitations have been sent out already. Tomorrow is the engagement ceremony and both our families will be there, and tomorrow I must move into what will become my married house." He sighed, and a strange, almost religious expression crept into his eyes and his voice trembled with the awesome sanctity of the event. "So you see, tomorrow I have to make my promise, on my honour, and then exchange rings. It is a very solemn and serious undertaking. I am truly, truly sorry Lauren."

Lauren was too stunned to say anything to begin with. She considered it from several angles, but from whatever perspective the sense of 'honour' he had just mentioned seemed to jar.

"Tell me, from the way *you* look at things, have these last three days with me been *honourable* for you in regard to your future wife?"

"Aah, I see what you mean... No, not honourable; but also not dishonourable, because I've yet to make my solemn promise to her."

"You must have made personal promises though, just as you did to me. *So,* I think I'm beginning to understand it now. You gambled on the chance that I *wouldn't get a job.* Am I right? You felt sure you'd get away with it... Tomorrow I'd be on my way back to England in happy ignorance, while you'd be slipping on that ring like a true, noble gentleman, uttering your promise with a clear conscience! But what I *still* don't understand is, if you Italian men really take these vows so very seriously, how comes most married Italians go chasing after other girls? Or are you a rare serious type, which somehow I failed to notice?"

Paolo looked a little more cheerful with this distinction. "The vows you make on engagement are more solemn and more serious than those you make on marriage," he declared earnestly. Then his look of assurance faded, "Well, it might be that or, because marriage lasts such a very long time, perhaps the strength of the vows starts to fade... Or you perhaps begin to tire of your wife." It was amazing, really, how well his brain operated once it could shift into self-justification gear.

"Obviously I can't complain," Lauren spoke as if she too were thinking aloud, "since you owe *me* nothing. In fact you've looked after me very well, and I'm grateful for that. If you'd told me the truth straight away we'd have skipped out the sex, and I guess you wouldn't have bothered to look after me *without* the sex, so I can see your reasoning there. And the sex was quite fun, most of the time. What I *can't* fully understand though, is why tell all those gratuitous lies about the future? Why promise all those wonderful things we'll do over the summer and pretend how much you love me? You didn't need to say *any* of it... Is it a kind of obligatory soundtrack you need in order to perform properly?"

Paolo stared at her aghast. "How can you be so cold Lauren? So matter of fact? I am feeling truly terrible and yet you - who are so much younger - are so unemotional. Not a single tear in your eye! Don't you...don't you care about me *at all*?"

Lauren laughed cheerfully, "I don't know how you manage to always turn things around! Yes, I do feel upset, but not because of jealousy like you want - only because I've been cheated - in the sense of being taken in by your story. I hate being made a fool of. I *should* have suspected of course; that I didn't is what annoys me."

Paolo sat with his head in his hands, having drunk his wine much too fast instead of savouring it as he had repeatedly assured her was the better way, the Italian way. The English were such an unfeeling people; Lauren had arrived so forlorn, unloved and uncared for - even downright grubby. He had treated her like a film star, toasted her, escorted and protected her and given her all those wonderful gifts of love and flattery. Yet now, simply from being caught out in a little romantic peccadillo of such understandable rationale, she somehow seemed to have snatched the upper hand and stolen his authority. How *had* he let that happen? *He* should be the one feeling proud, the man in charge at the apex of a love triangle, the object of desire fought over with tears and torment by the two women he had courted and flattered so exceedingly well.

"How shall we sleep tonight?" he asked, with a sniff to convey his utter disinterest.

"Well it's *your* bed," Lauren answered fairly, "but there again it's also *your* floor...Why don't we toss for it?"

"Er, OK. What with?"

"Why not the ring?"

"*Lauren!* But it's perfectly round. If it falls one way or the other, it's exactly the same. It will tell us nothing."

"Sounds symbolically perfect. Spin it, if it falls to the right you get the bed, to the left I do."

"From whose point of view? We're sitting opposite each other."

"Choose north or south then."

"South."

Lauren grinned triumphantly, "I knew you would."

But after winning the toss she confused him all the more by choosing to sleep on the floor, for she claimed this was the only position in which she could possibly still look up to him. It also reminded her of the happy days she had spent with Merle and Florentina, so she told him about them while they waited for sleep to come.

"*American lesbians?*" Paolo's voice resonated with equal horror and contempt. "Lauren! You should *never* have taken such a terrible risk! Lesbians are sad, dangerous, embittered women because they are unfulfilled. They have never known a *real* man."

Lauren could not help smiling secretly in the darkness.

Before she left to meet Signora Martinelli she thanked him profusely for his wonderful hospitality, which truly could not be faulted, and he graciously offered her the services of his friend Emilio to escort her places in lieu of him on her days off from her au pair duties, since she would certainly need an escort.

"Emilio? Isn't he the very shy, freckled one we met at the bar? So he's no threat to your pride then, but what's in it for him?"

"He's head over heels in love with you Lauren, yet accepts he has no chance. It would be an honour for him."

"Honour is a word we understand differently, I think. So tell me, why do you need him to spy on me?"

"It's not that remotely, not at all, amore mio."

"You can skip the 'amore' now, remember."

"Of course there's no question of spying!" He blushed with the outrage.

The Martinellis treated her like one of the family, so that by the end of the summer, which was also the tail end of her gap year before going to University, she had an almost fluent grasp of Italian.

But, she told herself with a wry smile, she still had lots more to learn about the vagaries of human nature, and there were no courses or au pair jobs to help with that. It would probably take a whole lifetime, and even at the end you could never count on being able to understand it fully.

The Back Burner

The midday sun blazed down. First it evaporated all the splash-pools of spray flung onto the rocks at high tide, leaving dry, flaky smears of salt crystals in their place; then it scorched the rocks with such ferocity that their colours bleached away.

If you touched the rocks it seared your skin. And the sandy beach was worse - it burned like smouldering coals, bubbling and blistering the soles of your feet. Even if you emerged dripping wet from the sea, this only delayed the burning effect for a few extra seconds.

Some man full of bravado thought he could beat the heat and complete the hundred metre sprint from shoreline to esplanade. It was simply a matter of persevering through the pain, was his theory. However, not being an eastern holy man who could meditate and walk on glass but a fat Brit with a beer belly, he collapsed about halfway towards his finish line. Some said the soles of his feet had melted into beeswaxy shreds and he had passed out from the pain; others - compelled by curiosity to rush over and watch the paramedics - that it was the sheer extremity of pain which brought about a heart attack that had been waiting its pretext to happen.

His condition must have been serious because the ambulance crew urgently loaded his unconscious body on board and drove off with flashing lights, and he never reappeared on the beach, neither that day nor any other. The event therefore grew in importance and remained a topic of conversation amongst beach goers for quite a while.

Apart from the man who had dived - for a laugh - from a twelfth storey balcony after too many shots of tequila, confusing the ornate circular fountain below with the deep end of the hotel swimming pool, it was *the* cautionary tale of that August tourist season.

Aaron drowsed lazily on his aquamarine beach towel, wondering what exactly it was that impelled certain men into performing such death-defying acts. Not that the syndrome was exclusively a male one, for a particular breed of female ladette could just as easily become addicted to the adrenalin rush they got from this sort of exhibitionist daredevilry.

He had *never* been tempted, not even remotely. He preferred to lead his simple, low key life, savouring peace and relative anonymity. It was for this very reason he had remained a little-known stage actor who specialized in minor supporting roles. Prominent lead roles, all that slavering after publicity and hankerings for fame and fortune, had never been a serious lure.

Even basic comfort was not necessary, he decided. So although his towel was right now impregnated with fine grains of sand that sharply grazed his skin like glass splinters whenever he shifted his position - to the extent that he had red friction burns and scratches where it had rubbed - he could still relax, close his eyes and listen to the wonderfully soporific sounds of the sea. The soft smacking of lips as the wavelets kissed the shore and the hiss as the water sucked back, then broke again on the smooth wet sand. He could absorb the warmth of the sun and melt into his surroundings just as naturally as the foam from the breaking waves dissolved to creamy bubbles along the shoreline, and he could switch off from all the noises - shrieking kids, couples arguing, distant police sirens, beach pedlar's prattle - just by wishing to.

He lay relaxed and still until runnels of sweat coolly tickled his ribs. Then, with an involuntary shiver he abruptly sat up, afflicted by a sudden, unexpected restlessness.

The mounting heat had created a mirage so that the now-liquid rocks seemed to sway and the sand vibrate, pockmarked here and there by pools of shining mercury, while the sea shimmered blindingly with flecks of silver and light. But despite all these dizzying, swirling movements caused by the mirage he had this strange, unpleasantly claustrophobic sensation that the spinning world had, without any warning whatsoever, bizarrely ceased to either rotate or revolve.

He reoriented himself by staring fixedly at the sea until his alarmingly warped perception readjusted itself. It was not the world itself that was static, he now realised, just his own *private, personal world.* His thoughts continued in this irrational vein, but in addition to the sensation of a non-revolving world that gyrated like some drunk lurching about, he now had an even weirder feeling. And it was this: that *the essence of his future life* (and he neither believed in 'essences' nor ever indulged in future thinking, or not normally) had just slunk past him while he lay innocently lost in thought upon the sand! Worse still, its attitude to him was contemptuously dismissive; it had glanced at him witheringly, frowning irritably at his prostrate body on its rumpled towel. What *could* that mean? Well, nothing pleasant, that was for sure. In fact the most obvious interpretation would be…that it had just consigned him to an imminent, premature death!

Quick as a flash he hunted for his badly stretched T-shirt and flung it over his head like a hood. Paranoia induced by sunstroke - that must be his problem. The exact reason cautious, sensible people wore sunhats. He badly needed water too, for he could detect a nasty incipient headache from the dehydration. How stupid he had been to lie roasting in the noonday sun. *'Mad dogs and Englishmen…'* Too late he remembered the age-old refrain.

Immediately he rejected his previous pretence of inner harmony and oneness with the universe, plus all the other self-delusory ideas he had been entertaining. Instead he suddenly and emphatically deplored sunbathing because - as he had always known - it was both extremely unhealthy *and* deadly boring. He had never enjoyed the look or feel of his tanned skin anyway, so suffering to acquire a tan made no sense at all.

Galvanised, he stood up, gathered his gritty towel, dusty shorts and unread holiday book on the plight of the Maori population circa 1856, and plodded on slippery plastic flip-flops along the slatted wooden pathway (running barefoot, you see, had not simply been mad bravado but also completely unnecessary). He headed straight for the shady avenue formed by two parallel lines of parasols made from thatched twigs - presumably to invoke a South Sea Island feel, for the waiting canoes at six Euros an hour had likewise been painted in vulgar imitation of the style of Gauguin.

He paid three Euros for a canvas deckchair with a rickety foot extension, then shook his towel with meticulous care to remain downwind from the adjoining deckchairist, who looked powerfully built so not the type to smother in sand; then settled down to drink thirstily from a half-litre bottle of chilled mineral water.

The drink and the beautiful round pool of deep shade brought him immediate relief from the heat and glare, but they failed to banish his new mood of depression. For now the thought struck him that although sunbathing was a waste of time and obviously physically harmful, it was not of itself boring. In fact if you shut away the outside world to concentrate on your inner thoughts and that leaves you bored - well then, it must be *you* who is boring!

It seemed so bitterly ironic that there he was, busily congratulating himself for not dying through the need to show off, only to then have his brief moment of holiday contentment (and he had not had a proper holiday in years) insidiously eroded by self-doubt. Because he knew perfectly well they were but two sides of the same coin, introversion/extroversion, arrogant over-confidence/pathetic lack of it...both were profoundly egocentric - and he had not one iota of sympathy for that state.

Too many of his gay friends periodically and pointlessly beat themselves up over their sexuality; deeply questioning their urges, desires, orientations and vagaries of taste. He had never indulged in such pointless interrogations, nor in the consequent rewards or punishments (which he suspected were the real attraction anyway). He simply accepted that he was gay and got on with his life. It made no difference to him whether it was due to his genes, his hormones, his family background, his mother or his schooling. It just *was* and did not especially bother him. Even for this particular, long-overdue holiday he had not chosen a specifically gay destination, not Thailand or Hawaii or Bali or that more subtle, low profile resort in Menorca that was the latest place in vogue. Nor had he even so much as *inquired* about gay bars or discos where he was, so that showed how little he was motivated by any form of sexual activity to enliven his holiday.

Rest and relaxation were all he desired. Celibacy was honestly a preference. But *not* depression!

Unable to concentrate on the Maoris and their tragic lack of immunity to the measles virus imported by their vicious European invaders, he squeezed his feet into his brand new pair of flippers which still carried their dayglo price tag and swam straight out to sea, only turning parallel to the coastline when he was at least a quarter of a mile out. There was no shark net, so he surmised there *should be* no sharks. It was only that the deeper water further out turned several degrees colder and the tight grip of the rubber flippers seemed to hinder circulation, so that he was gradually aware that his feet - especially his little toes - were turning numb. Upon that thought he immediately found himself looking down to reassure himself they were still correctly attached to his body, for he was uncomfortably mindful of the little ironies of the day. If the pattern were to repeat itself then merely to *think* about sharks would be to invite them alongside.

Because the feet generated propulsion when swimming - just as the propeller drives a ship - he decided to head back towards the shore before the numbness became absolute and therefore a serious hindrance.

But here again he was bamboozled. Instead of the comforting ease with which he had swum out, however forcefully he now strained his muscles to reduce the growing distance between himself and the beach, he made no progress. It was in fact counterproductive. All the miniature dots of people with their colourful pinpricks of beach paraphernalia instead of growing actually shrank in size, and with each flurry of strokes they receded further! He was, it seemed, fated to bob helplessly like a discarded cork swept out to sea.

Was there, perhaps, some subterranean river canalised and buried beneath the artificial sand of the beach, that resurfaced and was now carrying him away on its current? Or was he (he grimaced in distaste) too near to the outlet for the municipal sewage pipe that was being pumped out to sea with a turbo-generated force? If there *was* such a sewage pipe, it would certainly disgorge at a safe distance from the beach so as to outwit those troublesome sanitary inspectors, giving lawsuit friendly tourists-types absolutely no grounds for complaint.

He decided to tread water. No point getting exhausted to no avail. Better to use his brains before they too turned numb. He now discarded both sewage and river theories in favour of an aberrational feature of the sea itself: an unusually powerful ebb tide, an offshore swell, or a notoriously dangerous undertow.

There *should* have been warning notices on the beach of course, and perhaps there had been - but because of his strange mental preoccupations he had foolishly blanked them out.

He groaned inwardly but mastered the reflex to panic. All was not *yet* lost. He was still physically (if not emotionally) buoyant and had not yet succumbed to hypothermia - apart from in the toes that is. There was still the chance of rescue. Perhaps that fit looking young coastguard who had been sitting high up on his aerial perch, his ears plugged into the heavy metal sounds of his ipod and his eyes closed so as to fully savour its aggressive rhythms, whose *only* job was to listen out for and watch for the safety of swimmers, had already noticed the fast vanishing blob of his head and his urgently waving arms, and had summoned the lifeboat crew. Fat bloody chance!

Or perhaps he would be swept onto the welcoming beach of a small offshore island, or conveniently close to a fishing boat or ocean liner - but not dangerously so, for their propeller blades were more lethal than any marine predator.

Perhaps...perhaps... perhaps... If he was to be perfectly honest with his perhapses, he should never have stupidly swum straight out to sea without taking stock of the local currents.

Whilst his mind flitted over the different aspects to a watery grave; whether sharks were like vultures and would touch dead flesh or, like tigers, preferred the fresh blood of the living; and where his body might ultimately end up, Africa or Europe, he gradually became more attuned to the shifts in the surface behaviour of the sea.

It now seemed to him that the offshore current was confined to the centre of the bay, where he could clearly see the seething, boiling and flecking of its deeper indigo waters, whereas directly beneath the steep overhanging cliffs of the headland on the north side of the beach was an area of calmer, achingly pale turquoise water that looked to be contrastingly still as a mill pond.

With a flicker of optimism, he turned his nose in the direction of those cliffs and flapped his flippers with renewed vigour.

Sometimes he thought he was making marvellous progress, but sometimes he feared it was a trick of perspective that deluded him like those deceptive mermaid songs of old (did they bother seducing sailors who were gay?). After half an hour's steady swimming, however, the cliffs loomed irrefutably closer. So much so that he was no longer fighting the tide but being firmly assisted by an inward drift carrying him straight towards their protective overhang, and he would have whooped with delight had he not noticed how viciously razor sharp they were. Every inch of their surface was smothered by infestations of sharply pointed limpet shells, and every hollow bare of *them* was bristling with the black spikes of sea urchins. Still, it was comforting to know that the worst he would now suffer was lacerations and infected splinters, which was vastly preferable to death.

The rock was a type of sandstone, whose vaulted arch formed by the overhanging cliffs had been gradually carved out by the steady erosion of the sea (with a sudden acceleration of damage when the Greek island of Santorini exploded from a mega-volcanic eruption). Thus a kind of natural walkway had been sculpted along the base of the cliff. At low tide it was fully exposed, but right now it was submerged by shallow water - no more than six to ten inches in depth.

After several failed attempts Aaron at last managed to scramble out onto this watery walkway without losing life-threatening quantities of blood, and since there was nowhere to sit and rest (owing to sea urchins etc.) he began to plod laboriously around the headland towards the beach. He made slow, wearying progress because the extra help and speed flippers give you when swimming has to be doubly subtracted when paddling in shallow water - and trebly so if you are already exhausted - but he dared not take them off and expose his bare feet to the mercies of limpets etc.

When he eventually limped and gasped his way back to the deckchair, the man in charge refused to let him rest on it. It transpired that since he had only paid for two hours, and because a total of four had now elapsed all his possessions: towel, book and clothes, had been confiscated as surety for the balance owed, just in case he never returned! Even when the man witnessed the horrifying rainbowed state of his skin, which was blue from cold, pink from sunburn, crimson from lacerations, and elsewhere a grimy white and horribly wrinkled from too long immersed in salty water, his expression was of disgust more than sympathy.

He *did* manage to dredge up some vague vestige of concern when Aaron tried in pigeon Italian to explain that he had been swept halfway to Tunisia, which was why he could only pay for *one* extra hour, not two, having not brought much money onto the beach. But the concern was only for the money, not Aaron. He made an unkind grab for the flippers, miming that Aaron would get them back once he paid the final balance of one Euro, 50 centimos. It was only when he spied their battered, mangled condition that he thrust them back, gesturing magnanimously that he was prepared to waive the debt. Aaron noticed with amazement that the price tag had miraculously survived - and better than the flippers; it had lost its dayglo colour but still hung bravely on by the slenderest of threads.

Three hours later Aaron felt blissfully recovered. He had showered and applied a whole tube of calendula cream to his cuts and scratches, which had smarted in the harsh salt water but now felt soothed. He was pleasurably exhausted and thoroughly pleased to still be alive, and was therefore able to resume his friendly inner dialogue with himself on the numerous and undoubted benefits of holidays. Sometimes one needed shocks and intimations of mortality to regain a proper perspective on life, he reminded himself. The events of the day *should* have warned him of the dangers of self-congratulation, of course, but he was hopelessly smug in the foolish assumption that the worst was past.

He was busy savouring a capuccino, *much* too late in the day according to his normal regimen (but he felt his marathon exertions would guarantee sleep no matter what dosage of caffeine he imbibed) when a terrifying thought struck him. When he had drunk his morning coffee before the airport taxi arrived, before his holiday properly began…*had or hadn't* he remembered to turn off the back burner of his gas cooker? Oh God - supposing he hadn't! *Surely* he would have made a conscious effort to check, after forgetting to do so on several previous occasions, and each time making an urgent mental note to check more thoroughly next time.

The only reason why this carelessness, this lapse in attention occurred was because, for his *second* cup of the day, he always decanted the coffee from his percolator to heat in a saucepan. He was very fastidious about this; coffee and milk *must* be heated separately because the milk should boil and froth but the coffee most assuredly should not - and the means by which he ensured that the coffee heated slowly to coincide *perfectly* with the milk was to have the gas flame on minimum. And the terrible danger with that was the vastly increased risk of leaving the flame on, because it was barely noticeable.

Suddenly all colour drained from his face. Feverishly he wound back the clock, revisited his kitchen and re-enacted his coffee making actions over and over again, but each time he reached the vital moment when he *should* have switched off that back burner his memory blacked out!! He cursed himself for ordering this capuccino when he could have calmly sipped tea or downed a modest half-pint of lager; it had merely agitated his frayed nerves and prompted fears that would have otherwise lain dormant.

With nervously tapping fingers and a fluttering, somersaulting stomach he left the bar and wandered disconsolately back to the hotel. He would have to curtail his holiday now, because unless he could be fully reassured he had turned off the gas he would not have another moment of peace.

He had been away four days. What were the possible scenarios, supposing the back burner *was* left on? Would the flame stay alight, gradually, inexorably heating up the metal rack and above that the extractor hood until both began to melt and buckle, soon fusing with something more flammable - something plastic or rubber (like the electrical wiring in the hood), until the whole kitchen caught fire with a terrifying whoosh? Or, would the minor draught from the air vent in his kitchen window eventually shift - with the change in prevailing wind direction, or a sudden blustery gust - so as to extinguish the flame, leaving a slow but steady leaking of gas?

He first toyed with the idea of phoning Mrs Beatty, his friendly neighbour who had a key to his basement flat. He could ask her to check that all was in order. He thought yearningly of her friendly words of reassurance. It tempted him beyond belief - but how could he possibly risk her life? If the gas *was* escaping she might collapse in the passageway, and be dead before anyone in the area noted the smell of gas and the suspicious open doorway from which it escaped. In his imagination he could clearly picture her large, matronly body sprawled lifeless upon his threadbare Axminster runner.

His now tremulous nostrils even fancied they were inhaling the sickly fumes of escaping gas from the separating distance of more than a thousand miles.

Or, what if the gas had already been escaping for *two or three days*? He had naturally left all the windows shuttered, bolted and barred, so there would be no dilution from the fresh outside air. The puny ventilation disks in both kitchen and bathroom barely did any ventilating, so by now a truly lethal concentration of gas would have accumulated. It would be so fiendishly concentrated that anyone within a radius of a hundred metres, simply by lighting a cigarette, would set off a mammoth explosion. And even if, against all odds, the entire neighbourhood had miraculously said no to smoking, there remained the alternative hazard of mobile phones. They apparently emitted sparks of radiation because he had read such a theory on warning notices at petrol pumps, and there was precisely *no chance* his neighbours would have renounced their addiction to mobile phones.

His complexion veered from bright pink (from the ravages of sun, sand and salt water) to a sickly green. Suddenly he could all-too-clearly visualise the imposing four storey Victorian building exploding like a mega-bomb, and he cowered in fear and guilt before the horrific vision.

His mind trembled too with other disastrous alternatives… Supposing the flame *had* remained 'on' so no gas escaped, well, the possibilities were scarcely better. A localised fire beginning in the kitchen would spread within minutes to the floor above, then engulf the whole building. Oh God *what a reckless, careless fool he'd been!* How had he *dared* to criticise that poor man who ran barefoot across hot sand and caused only self-harm, when *he* had so negligently endangered the lives of a huge, densely populated neighbourhood - and from the safe distance of over a thousand miles away.

On a desperate impulse he reached for his bedside telephone and feverishly dialled his home number, insanely allowing relief to flood through him when he heard it ringing healthily loud and clear. But his relief was short-lived. He soon collected his wits sufficiently to remember it was *not* the handset that rang, reassuringly informing him that the plastic phone was not a charred and molten mess amongst the ashes and fallen masonry. The dormant, rational sphere of his brain sadly kicked in to remind him of the sad truth that it was of course the central exchange that rang, not a friendly little bell tucked inside the handset!

Soon his humane, honest feelings of guilt began to fade; replaced by more dishonest ones of how to cover up his guilt. Supposing the building *did* burn down or blow up, those horribly officious inspectors who work for the police or insurance companies, if not both, would sift through the rubble and find evidence that indisputably attributed the cause to his gas burner. And once they did, his insurance would cruelly refuse to pay because it was his own careless fault, so outside their terms of liability. He would be bankrupted! And…and…if anyone was injured, or God forbid - killed, he would also be *criminally* liable! He shivered, imagining with crystal clarity the rows of homophobes crowding the public gallery in court, jeering and cheering as he was led off to serve the maximum sentence for culpable manslaughter.

He survived a sleepless night, somehow or other. He was utterly alone in his misery, for he dared not phone a single friend or neighbour to ask them to check whether the building was still standing. For - supposing it was not - to do so would immediately incriminate him. Whereas if he arrived back and looked as shocked and surprised as anyone *would* be - and in that kind of twitchy, highly strung role his acting prowess always made him truly convincing in - there was a chance they might be clumsy enough to overlook the real cause and erroneously blame some old, decrepit length of lead piping for the gas leak.

He utterly despised this miserable, cowardly, deceptive, false position he had slithered into, but sadly he had fallen so low in self-esteem he could not argue his way out of it.

As soon as the first streaks of an early dawn brightened the night-sky he dialled the airline, requesting they switch his return ticket to the first available seat on any plane to any airport in southern England. By this stage he no longer cared whether foreshortening his holiday looked suspicious because, overwhelmed by terror, continuing the role of carefree tourist was unthinkable - despite being a pro at method acting.

For better or worse, he *had* to know if the back burner was left alight.

When he reached the airport the queue snaking back from the distant check-in counter looked ominously long. Gritting his teeth to prevent them chattering, he silently prayed this backlog of passengers did not signify a delay. Or, worse still, a cancelled flight.

He tagged onto the back of the queue. Every noise jarred and the general mood of cheeriness intensified his alarm. Kids encircled him, hopping and skipping in frenzied glee, glowing and healthy after two weeks in the sun and bubbling with the excitement of going home to their usual food and familiar TV programmes. Their parents were equally horrendous - exchanging raucous jokes and reminiscences, vying with each other in booming voices over who had had the funniest, most idyllic, most perfect of holidays. But at least their plumper frames persuaded them from *physical* bounciness.

Despite his sense of urgency he allowed one group to supersede him in the queue, giving up what might prove to be the last available seat on an overbooked flight, simply in order to tuck in behind an old grandma who looked suitably grim and as near to death's door as anyone can be whilst still allowed to fly, just because her forbidding expression made her a kindred spirit. Was he forever fated to be at odds with the crowd? What sort of cruel, linguistic irony had sprung up to equate being homosexual with being 'gay', for heaven's sake?

At last the queue began to shuffle forwards. It took twenty minutes for him to reach the desk, during which time he passed through stages of hysteria (silent ones, no screaming) until he entered a strange state of numbness that was surprisingly peaceful. A number of sea urchin spines were still implanted in his body - in personal places where he could neither inspect nor extract them, and he wondered if the sensation of euphoria came from some anaesthetic substance they gave off.

Despite the frenzy of his hotel departure he had managed to grab the crucial things like passport and original return ticket, so his total absence of luggage (which he *had* forgotten) need arouse no suspicion because he could pretend he travelled light by choice. He also felt reassured that his haunted face and all the other obvious signs of a sleepless night - hollow eyes, shaking hands, sweating forehead etc., would simply be misconstrued as typical tourist symptoms after a blinder of a final night on the town.

Fortunately his seat was next to grandma's. She had no more wish to converse than he did, being too busy coping with her breathing (asthma? weak heart?), and Aaron for once was not bothered by his usual fear of flying, since if they were to crash he would mercifully avoid the consequences of whatever destruction he had caused back home.

Instead he stared dazedly at the wrinkled sea far below, reflecting how teasingly it had toyed with his body only yesterday, and how happy he had felt when it had spared his life…and how brief had been those moments of joyful celebration before his current nightmare struck.

But time moves ever onward and space adjusts; next he found himself no longer airborne but sitting in the rear of a taxi. Not, however, on a palm-lined Mediterranean boulevard on the way to the airport as he had been several hours ago, but tucked behind a van on a clockwise lane of the north circular, waiting bleakly for a red light to turn green somewhere near Wembley. Twenty minutes from home. From confronting the truth...

Escape beckoned temptingly. An irresponsible impulse urged him to simply keep on travelling. *This,* it argued, was his golden opportunity to visit long-lost friends, see that distant cousin on Dartmoor who had been inviting him for years, even call on his aged aunt in Weymouth who had long ago forgotten who he was. Just *in case* he decided to obey it he had given the taxi driver his nearest tube station as his destination, not his actual address. The man had already delivered him a terrifying jolt with some idle chit-chat about a recent closure of the north circular due to a fire - but it turned out to have been a timber mill near Brent Cross, so his heart was able to resume pumping once more.

The taxi duly dropped him off half a mile from his real destination. He dallied there as a delaying tactic; bought bread, butter, milk, and extra-strong mints from the corner shop. He gobbled the entire packet whilst walking towards his flat, hoping they would focus his mind and override the taste of fear. Occasionally he sniffed at the air and wondered if the noxious cocktail of fumes he was inhaling contained the sickly, deadly ingredient of gas. But the nauseous undertone was actually diesel, he decided, set against the sharper, more uniform stench of differing octane petrol fumes.

He stopped for a while at the entrance to his road, shifting from foot to foot, prolonging the moment as long as possible. *I'm a coward*, he whispered, but that long established, self-evident truth failed to goad him beyond the final corner.

At last he coaxed his reluctant legs into motion. Incredibly, from the far end of the street, the house appeared to be fully intact (unless the explosion had only ripped through the rear façade leaving the front unharmed, a 2D illusion like the backdrop to a theatre set), and all the pedestrians passed it by as nonchalantly as every other terraced frontage to either side. He stumbled twice, not from the disorienting effects of gas-laden air but due to lack of sleep. Could...could he *dare to hope?* He reached the wrought iron staircase leading to the basement door on the far side of the building. *Still* an air of normality reigned - and the air was no more contaminated than it habitually was from the nearby rubbish bins.

It was only when he actually placed his key in the lock that he had the sensation all was not as he had left it; that an indefinable *something* had changed.

It made the hairs on the nape of his neck bristle as he stepped inside. His breath quickened, his throat restricted - not from gas fumes but from the instinctive knowledge that *someone was in there!* The surge of hostility combined with a feeling of awful suspense. But, thanks God, the unfamiliar, faintly perfumed atmosphere told him that whoever was hiding there was assuredly still alive! He could almost *hear* them listening to the creak of the opening door, to his foot brushing the doormat, hear their fear at his sudden intrusion. A squatter? A burglar (hopefully in the singular!)? Or Mrs Beatty helping herself to a rare moment of peace, whilst he was abroad and out of the way?

Suddenly, galvanised, he strode along the corridor towards the sitting room, noting en route from the corner of an eye the miraculously intact cooker (that had so nightmarishly haunted him for sixteen long hours), and a cut glass vase bulging with vulgar russet chrysanthemums. The hated flowers gave him a fleeting warning of the possible identity of his uninvited guest.

"Aaron?" her voice was *almost* tentative, even timid - despite her having the advantage of knowing whose flat she was occupying, whereas he was thrown completely off balance because her intrusion was more unlikely than any proverbial month of Sundays.

Flooded by an intense relief that he was *not* a mass murderer he could almost have wept with joy. But simultaneously he felt sick, as if an iron fist had powered into his abdomen, because his peaceful, private world had been invaded by the one person he thought he had escaped for ever. The only individual in a cruel world who had *always* spelled darkness and misery, had always goaded, undermined and condemned him for who he was…

"Mum?" he asked wearily. Since he knew the answer already it was a purely rhetorical device, a tactic to preserve some vestige of politeness before the poison inevitably spilled.

"So - slinking back three days ahead of schedule then? I might've guessed you wouldn't cope… 'N they say the fags is cheaper out there too!" she chuckled mirthlessly at the brilliance of her wit.

He did not bother to reply. Poor unsuspecting Mrs Beatty must have given her the key, he guessed, and told her how long he expected to be away. How was the poor dear to know how badly he and his mother got on?

"What made you come *here*?" He tried to make it sound casual, almost bored, as if she frequently popped in for a tea bag or a spoonful of salt. Yet they had in truth neither seen each other nor exchanged so much as a word in over eleven years.

She was uncharacteristically silent, as if she had genuinely forgotten why she had come. Perhaps she *had* changed, he thought hopefully. Perhaps those eleven years had taught her the value of silence, that if there are things you cannot change in another then the endless stream of taunting and the bitterness have only a negative effect. What you cannot alter you should leave alone.

"I'd nowhere else to go. Yer bloody dad's walked out on me Aaron, after all these years. I...I...couldn't stand being on me own."

He stared at her bewildered. Dumbstruck at finally hearing the words he had been eternally amazed *not* to have heard ever since about the age of six - or whenever it was that he was old enough to realise that his dad hated her, but for some obscure reason lacked the will to leave her.

All the recent turmoil of rehearsing his shock-horror on seeing the blasted shell of his ruined flat buried by rubble, and all through the long, agonised hours fearing he had left the gas flame alight - and therefore kept hearing the haunting screams of his victims, and the wail of sirens as the ambulances ferried the few desperate survivors to hospital...none of it seemed to have prepared him for this very different bombshell of a surprise.

She sat there, a vast stone slab, confronting him with her inscrutable fat backside, refusing to turn and look at him. Come to think of it she had always avoided eye contact, except in extreme moments of apoplectic, red-eyed rage.

Then, to his bewildered consternation, her shoulders began to wobble jerkily with the effort of forcing back unshed tears, and he heard a harsh, rasping sound as she were trying to clear her throat of its unfamiliar, unwelcome lump of emotion. Oh God - he had *never* once seen his mother cry!

The interlude of silent sobbing was thankfully brief, and followed by the more familiar torrent of words. It was not her usual rant against men and minorities, however, but words she had kept pent up throughout her marriage. All through the long monologue her voice squeaked and cracked, pitching and falling in volume and register as if she were a teenage boy whose voice was breaking. His mind played vaguely with the idea that she was *at last* undergoing a sex change, a transformation that would come as no surprise to him at all.

Some of what she said flowed over him without him paying proper attention, but other parts sunk in deep.

"He never was yer dad, Aaron, much as you always listened to him more than me. Don't go telling him I told you though, 'cos he didn't want you told. (Though why I should care about his wishes after what's happened now, I really can't bloody fathom). *Why did he marry me?* I guess you must be wondering, seeing as there wasn't no love lost neither side - though I felt grateful enough to him for the first few years, I'm not too proud to admit that.

Yer real dad bummed off and left me in the lurch almost soon as he learned I was pregnant…but don't go thinking you'll get to see him and have a nice little cosy-up after all these years, 'cos the bastard's dead and good riddance, far as I heard, some time ago. And he never tried to find out about you, nor sent you so much as a sixpence, so don't get dewy eyed about *him,* it'd be a waste of finer feelings. Only reason yer dad (not yer real dad, Aaron, the one we lived with and I'm too much in the habit of calling him that to change now) wanted to marry me was for his own pride and safety. He was homosexual just like you, so you ought to understand it, only in them days it wasn't so fashionable and trendy like it is now, especially not down our neighbourhood.

He'd got in a right tizz about some gang of big bruisers calling him an effing fairy up at the local pub, plus not wanting to shock and shame his own parents, and in a daft moment, without bothering to think it properly through, he offered to marry me. Seemed like a good way out of a deep dark hole for me, 'cos I was deathly sick every morning and couldn't even think straight as a result. Also me dad would've kicked me out the house soon as he learnt I was an *'ignorant slut'* - as how he would've put it. And me mum would've cried herself to death if she couldn't give me a white wedding, seeing as she'd been planning that ever since she knew she couldn't have no more children and I was to be her only daughter.

Why didn't I tell you, you must be thinking. Well I think I might've, had it been down to me alone. But yer dad was adamant (I think you know which dad I mean). So on we go with the charade for years and years, he thinking he's done brilliant to scotch that silly rumour of being a flamin' fairy 'cos look: how *could* he be one - if he's been man enough to get a woman pregnant and have to marry her so as to make an honest woman out of her?

'Honest', what a bloody laugh! Not that we ever pretended to either love or fancy each other, at least we didn't fake *that.* You knew very well we got on each other's nerves and never even shared the same bed or

63

bedroom. We didn't act the loving couple for you or anyone, but it still seemed bloody daft that we couldn't tell you the truth when you was a bit older and had gone ahead and told us you yerself was screwed up sexually, so you wasn't in no position to be judgmental was you? - I think yer dad had this dumb idea you'd go blamin' *him* for yer preferences. Of course it never bloody occurred to him what it did to *my* bloody self-esteem being surrounded on all sides by men what found women repulsive, 'cos that's how I see it, despite you wanting to contradict."

Aaron wandered across the room to the tall casement window which overlooked his small back garden. He stood totally still, gazing absentmindedly out onto the brilliantly green handkerchief patch of lawn already bestrewn with the first falling leaves of Autumn. He caught a fleeting glimpse of the resident bushy tailed squirrel. It scurried along the top of the end fence with a curious undulating motion, one that was simultaneously jerky and yet gracefully smooth. Its movement had to be generated by the stabilising effect of its full and fluffy tail, he decided, for he had noticed that its close first cousin the rat, which periodically slunk up the canal bank to pilfer the rubbish bins by the basement steps, moved with a completely different gait - more of an odious slither, propelled by its thin, worm-like tail.

He himself had a strong déjà-vue sensation of floating once again on the vastness of the sea, swept along by the currents whither they wished and powerless to forge his own direction. His whole childhood faith, not in God of course, but in the certain knowledge that his father loved him whereas his mother only felt hatred, and that he correspondingly echoed and returned those exact same feelings, had suddenly broken anchorage and cast him dizzily adrift. From his recent rehearsal with the real sea he now knew that the pull of the tide was wayward and unpredictable; but if he trod water a while the time for reasserting control would quite possibly come.

Right now he felt the tug of a powerful ebb tide, - an entirely novel urge to sympathise with his mother, yet this untried wave of emotion only alerted his suspicious nature. For he knew her to be quite capable of any - if not *every* - form of trickery there was. If his dad *had* finally walked out on her she would, whatever the underlying truth, canvas Aaron's support and poison her rival's reputation just as viciously as she could.

Not having slept or had a moment's peace throughout the previous twenty four hours made it even harder for him to effectively collect his thoughts and fathom his true feelings.

However…supposing his mistrust and dislike of her had all along been unfounded? Perhaps it had been carefully introduced, and then oh-so studiously nurtured and compounded by a resentful father figure masquerading as his dad… Had he even been purposely *recruited* by his dad to hate her?

This was what he of course needed to understand - yet how on earth could he decide where the truth lay? He had obviously been duped, but since both of them had misled him did it really matter who had deceived him most? And did it really alter anything, if he wasn't who he thought he was - and nor were they? The rocks were splintery sharp, he remembered, but cutting yourself as you clambered out onto them was infinitely preferable to drowning in the watery depths of the sea.

"I guess you can stay here for a while mum," he allowed, "while you work out what to do next." He approached the sofa so as not to underline the still massive gulf between them. "But not for too long - seeing as you won't enjoy the company I sometimes keep."

"That's all I wanted Aaron," she treated him to her jowly profile, "I don't want to dump meself on you permanently. But you do owe me a bit of hospitality after what I've done fer you."

"You mean all that motherly love and the happy family atmosphere?" he couldn't yet manage to eliminate all the old sarcasm.

To his surprise she shrugged this off with a casual indifference and *almost* looked him in the eye - and with something uncannily close to a genuine smile.

"Nah, not for that you great dumbo," she said, "but because I got here in the bloody nick of time to turn yer gas off - which you'd gone and left merrily burning away like the cretin you are - and prevent the whole ruddy building getting blasted to bloody kingdom come!"

Two Fathers

Being in love blows common sense out of the window. It must do - or Ellie would never have deceived herself this visit home was a bright idea. The trouble with being romantically besotted is that you have this stupid notion your feelings are shared, illogically believing that the warm, rosy cocoon you both inhabit embraces everyone else. Before falling in love you were perfectly aware of the competitive, cruel streak in humanity; so why you ignore this and suddenly expect others to *enjoy* your euphoria and *celebrate* your good fortune is plain lunacy.

Especially if they happen to be your father, who will inevitably suspect you have chosen the wrong man...

Ellie was the youngest of the family, and her father's expectations had always lain heavily and uneasily on her narrow shoulders.

"Marry into money," went his rallying cry throughout her puberty years and beyond, "that is, if you want to carry on enjoying the same lifestyle, the one you know you're accustomed to. I simply don't have enough money to spread it decently between the four of you."

He seemed to feel that she owed him to marry 'well', her older sisters having all forged links that were deemed unsatisfactory, one way or another. The eldest had married a divorcee at least ten years her senior, but all the money he pretended to have prior to the marriage had been successfully channelled off by the bright young spark of a lawyer his ex-wife had hired to extract maximum maintenance, so that they now lived morosely in a one bedroom flat in an ugly part of Golders Green. The second sister had unforgivably 'gone foreign' (*and* downhill socially) by marrying a French chef from Marseilles, then vanishing to wash his pans and dishes in a roadside *routier* somewhere deeply remote in the Massif Central, never to be heard from again. The third now ran a stray cats' home in Weybridge, and the undeniable masculinity of her long-term female companion forced Ellie's father to abandon any hope of getting her to marry even the wrong type of man. So that left Ellie to fulfil the sum total of his hopes, dreams and paternal ambitions.

He must surely have known that his matchmaking fantasies were out of touch and out of date, owing to the social revolution that had been gathering momentum since the early sixties, and was now - in the early seventies - as firmly rooted as the clump of stinging nettles that he attacked with a mattock every Spring, and which grew back defiantly and always smothered his delicate clumps of yellow celandines.

However he was one of the very last babies born in the dying throes of the nineteenth century, and he clung to his strict Victorian values and mores like the proverbial drowning man to his straw. He had managed to bring up the three older girls in a reasonably correct, conventional manner, with pre-school nannies, a secluded boarding school education during their teens, and those fiendishly expensive finishing schools to add the final touches of sophistication - after which of course it all went horribly wrong.

Ellie was the only post war baby, so even finding her a suitable nanny had been a feat of Herculean difficulty. Thereafter he had tried his best to keep the reins of control and steer her upbringing within sensible perameters, but it all got out of hand due to those forces outside his influence: wild rock music, crazy clothes, hippies, the permissive society, women's lib, free love and all those other insidious freedoms.

As Ellie sat on the train seat watching the familiar landscape of her childhood rushing to meet her, she thought of all the earlier attempts her parents had made to link her up to the right kind of man. She had been wrapped in silk and taffeta and sent to eighteenth birthday and twenty-first 'coming out' balls, taught the rules of cricket and forced to watch the village first eleven on Sundays, and the most frequent attempts at matchmaking had been summer tennis parties with spotty youths from 'good' families lured in to partner her. She could even play tennis quite well, but because mini-skirts and hot pants were the latest fashion she and her partner always lost, for whichever spotty youth it happened to be invariably became distracted by her bare thighs into taking his eye off the ball just when he should have been smashing home a winner. In her memory their faces all blended into one hot, red, sweaty blob, below which an Adam's apple bobbled and bounced as if hungrily swallowing the tennis ball.

Syed was so unlike those shiny, steaming lobsters that he must *surely* appeal to her father's aesthetic sense - or so she convinced herself. And this testified to her love blindness; the usual mistaken idea lovers have that others will view their loved ones through their own captivated eyes. For her he was perfection itself. He was slim yet strong, neither too tall nor too short, had warm brown eyes and exquisitely sensitive hands, and he walked with the grace of a fallow deer (a male one, of course).

It did not seem to enter her head that her father's idea of masculine good looks was classic Edwardian. He considered long hair anathema, a fashion statement belonging to Neanderthal times. It was *just about* permissible in the Middle Ages (providing it was a wig on a bald pate of an aristocrat), but totally abhorrent in the modern era. And, to add insult to injury, Syed's hair was not just long but *dangerously dark,* while the blood that circulated so excitingly for Ellie beneath the flawless olive skin was alarmingly foreign in her father's opinion. It came direct from the Punjab and the equally terrifying mountainous Kashmir.

Even here Ellie was insanely naïve, for she actually hoped that mountains would prove a shared bond between them. Her father was a mountaineering fanatic - every August he scurried off to Switzerland for a fortnight of climbing and had a huge collection of ice-axes and walking sticks clattering about in his clothes cupboard as fond souvenirs.

She was not quite so crazed as to deceive herself that her loved one's career choice would bedazzle her father, who viewed dancing as a party thing and otherwise a girl's pastime, but she did rather bank on the fact that his *father's* career would redress the balance. Her father, after all, was an unrelenting snob and apart from being a genuine King, Emporer, Prince, Baron, Duke or Dictator, being an Ambassador was surely a cut above most things. She sort of hoped that her father would be so busy drooling over the Ambassador tag that he would barely notice the 'of Pakistan' tagged on at the end.

She stole a tender look at her loved one, who sat in rapt concentration on the opposite window seat surveying the self-same landscape unfold in reverse. Who could possibly fail to appreciate the fine curve of his eyebrows, the sculptural quality of his cheekbones and jaw? But as her eyes flickered downwards to his body she realised with alarm that he was wearing *her* sleeveless V-necked sweater, the daringly colourful one from *Mr Freedom,* which she had worn on her previous visit home so her father would be absolutely sure to recognise it - the more so because he had twice voiced disapproval of its brashness. She winced. An unwise choice. Her father would interpret it wrongly - concluding either Syed was too broke to buy his own clothes, or that he got kicks out of wearing hers. Also, it would tactlessly drive home their bodily closeness in ways fathers get uncomfortable with. Paranoia now taunted her into believing that the sweater had been visibly stretched by the curve of her breasts, and two pert-looking bulges marked the exact spot where her nipples had distorted the ribbing.

Syed sensed her anxious gaze and turned from the window to look at her. Although his smile was both genuine and reassuring, she could tell from the troubled expression in his eyes he already knew their visit was doomed. Her stomach contracted sharply as they decelerated into the station. And once the train shuddered to a halt they walked forlornly up the windswept stairs and left along a desolate corridor to the exit, neither of them willing to articulate their bewildered, synchronised thought, '*Why* did we come?'

Her father could be spotted pacing up and down the station foyer. His programmed smile tightened to a thin, mean line as he failed to disguise - even remotely - that his worst fears were realised. Her polite, well brought up lover gallantly proffered his hand in greeting, but her disapproving father deliberately ignored it. Muttering 'car park' he abruptly turned his back to march down the flight of stairs, leaving them to follow at his heels like a pair of well trained dogs. In hindsight they should have taken this cue to avoid further insult and caught the first returning train to London - leaving her father looking foolishly about himself when he reached his car and found himself alone. But sadly a feeling of numb ineffectiveness supplanted all intelligent thought, so that they glumly followed in her father's wake, programmed by birth and upbringing to mute and helpless filial obedience.

The front passenger door was opened for her, but Syed was left to find his own way into the back seat and probably meant to count himself lucky not to be stuffed into the rear section, which was segregated off by some stout wire mesh for the dogs.

Ellie sat in the front in a rising panic, unable to bridge the hostile wall of silence that had sprung up and uncertain what topic she should broach to dispel it. She knew her lover spoke eloquent, accent-less English, and could hold his own with anyone conversationwise as well as demonstrate his intelligence, given half the chance. But she had not banked on her father behaving so rudely that he would not be given that chance.

She felt ashamed. Reverting to her childhood self, she suffered the same humiliation she had faced after wetting the bed; the same palpitations of nervous guilt while she waited for the inevitable discovery of the crime.

It was her stepmother who finally broke the silence. She had never managed to keep her mouth shut and was doubtless incapable of the feat - even if her life depended on it. Ellie's mother had died several years ago and her father had, for a short period, tried to resist the pitfalls of remarriage, claiming to have rebuffed numerous flirtatious approaches from every eligible widow or spinster in the area. Ellie privately doubted the truth of this, for Daphne was a poor choice even for a desperate man in a field of one. It was more likely he had simply become sickened by his restrictive diet of boiled eggs, scrambled eggs and overdone steak, and saddened by the coldness of sleeping alone and the bleak monotony of his own company. Thus, in a weak moment, he had fallen easy prey to the wagging tongue of Daphne - who was cunning enough to know when to stop the flow of nonsense and whisper just the right flattering words to bamboozle an old man.

Or else he got drunk one night, and laid himself open to a charge of dishonour.

"My father was *awfully important* in Mysore," she announced proudly to Syed as she ushered them into the living room, "so I know *your part* of the world rather well. I've an old photo of me somewhere - riding an elephant to some Maharajah's palace."

Ellie did not dare look at Syed, who hated to be mistaken for Indian. Fortunately he already had plenty of experience of the middle class parents of school friends, so he knew that the full horror of being Asian was faintly redeemed by an Indian or 'Persian' label (the English were convinced these two stood aristocratically head and shoulders above the general riff-raff of eastern countries) so for the moment he let it go. He might also have been temporarily anaesthetised by the overwhelmingly strong smell of sherry that escaped her lips.

Daphne continued to fill the airwaves with her witterings about Maharajahs, elephants and jewels, and some ancillary story of serving girls and sewing which seemed to have no connection whatsoever to the main thread of her ramblings, until it was at last time for lunch. Seated around the table had a more confrontational aspect all of a sudden. It seemed to spur her father into paternal interrogation mode. Before a morsel had passed his lips he had sought to establish Syed's entire life history: date and place of birth (and their shocking reputation for unreliability), then parentage, schooling, university, future prospects etc.

Fortunately just before the awkward details of lack of money, love of dance and general romantic impracticalities could be touched upon, the job of eating rendered conversation impossible. The brace of roasted pheasant Daphne served up were so sinewy tough that rigor mortis must have somehow set in the very instant they were shot from the skies, and the so-called 'bread sauce' was so thickly glutinous it could be swapped with a latex-based wood glue and even a carpenter would be fooled.

As for the vegetable accompaniment, well, absolutely no-one in the world could massacre healthy brussel sprouts more thoroughly than Daphne - to the point that it was impossible to tell that they had ever been either green or growing. Thus they all, of necessity, became silently focused on emerging from the meal with tongue and teeth intact, and trying to ensure that the food was persuaded down the throat without the rebellious stomach rejecting it.

It was not until the pudding stage that words were possible again. Ellie knew that her father could be ridiculously pompous, yet a glass of wine or two during daylight hours usually made him mellower, earthier, less contrived. Not this time, however. The concept of heritage buildings had reared its unlikely head as a conversational topic, along with the exorbitant cost of restoring ancient treasures, when he suddenly turned on Syed and proclaimed;

> "Doubtless you have some rotting temples in the jungles of your native land?"

The words reverberated oddly in Ellie's ears. They were intoned in much the same declamatory style as he had always used when quoting stanzas from Coleridge's 'Kubla Khan' whilst buttoning up his shirts in his dressing room. But the way he spat out 'rotting' and 'native' was unquestionably derogatory, and Syed had the sharpest ears for insinuated insults. Quick as a flash he replied;

> "I'm afraid you're mistaken. You've got the wrong country. There are neither jungles nor temples in my *'native land'*."

Such an audacious riposte had a dramatic effect on Daphne. The previous moment she had been happily swallowing spoonfuls of sticky chocolate mousse in the rudest of health and as if wartime rationing had only recently been lifted; the next her face flushed an alarming deep, feverish purple, steam rose in wafts and she had to mop the sudden beads of sweat from her brow with an embroidered lace napkin.

> "Oh, I must to bed, my darling," she gasped hoarsely, "I should *never* have tried to stay up, what with this ghastly 'flu and my soaring temperature. I only did it to give you moral support."

And her emphasis on 'moral' so obviously implied that what went on between Ellie and Syed was anything but. At least her noisy, melodramatic departure, leaning heavily against Ellie's father's shoulder to prop her sagging body upright and steer her faltering footsteps in the direction of their bedroom, put paid to that particular conversational gambit. Ellie and Syed exchanged weary looks across the table.

"We might as well leave," Syed sighed, "They're not going to suddenly rethink their entire view of the world."

"I didn't think it'd be like this," Ellie murmured sorrowfully.

"I *did* try to warn you," Syed sounded faintly bitter.

She tried to restore some element of happiness by showing him her childhood haunts; the cherry trees and the plum orchard with its gnarled trunks, the broken treehouse in the weeping ash, the duck pond and winding footpath to the river where she used to hide as a child in the squat octagonal buildings called 'pill boxes' built during the war to repulse the anticipated hordes of invading Germans. She had always thought it stretched credulity to imagine anyone from a technically advanced era with aircraft and submarines would hatch an invasion plan that featured rowing tiny, flat bottomed rafts up small meandering rivers in Kent, but her father assured her you couldn't underestimate Germans - and it was anyway best to be prepared. Now it crossed her mind that, with just the same futility that these defensive bunkers had been built to repel a non-existent invasion, her father was staunchly arming himself against the imaginary evils of Syed.

When they returned from their walk her father, now unsmilingly hostile and stiff as a cardboard cutout, met them in the kitchen.

"Daphne'd like to see you. She's upstairs in bed," he snapped.

"Me - or both of us?"

"I think she'd like a word with you both," but he would not look her in the eye.

"I'm surprised she dares invite Syed into the privacy of her bedchamber," Ellie muttered bitterly.

Reluctantly they mounted the stairs and headed for the back bedroom, which used to be the guestroom before her mother died. Her father had at least had the decency to change beds on changing wives, Ellie thought grimly, coughing from the potent fumes wafting from Daphne's inhalation bowl, in which bouquets of eucalyptus leaves and bunches of peppermint swam disconsolately on the scummy surface.

Daphne's face was screwed in pain on the pillow, and thankfully a chunky bed jacket covered most of her transparent pink negligée. Nevertheless Ellie felt queasy at such close proximity to Daphne's flesh, while the double bed with her father's striped pyjamas peeking from beneath the adjacent pillow underlined the tactlessness towards her dead mother they both seemed utterly blind to. Daphne held out a limp hand, perhaps intending Ellie to squeeze it or Syed to shake it, but since neither could bring themselves to touch it it fell twitching onto the counterpane.

"I've telephoned my brother who's a topnotch MP," she whispered hoarsely. "He kindly checked with the FO, and it turns out Syed's story is actually true. His father *is* an Ambassador."

"The Foreign Office are highly unreliable," Syed declared, "It's a well known fact in diplomatic circles."

"How disappointing," Ellie said sarcastically, "I'd hoped he was a liar. That way he'd fit in with the family *so much better.*"

"Don't be so damned impertinent," her father interjected, having pursued them up the stairs. "Your stepmother's simply trying to help. You know *perfectly well* I'm displeased you're with a man...not...not...of your colour."

Ellie could hardly believe her ears, and it roused her into telling her own lie. One that she fervently hoped would not annoy Syed any more than he already was annoyed.

"Well you'd better get used to it because we're going to be married... After all, *you* just got married someone *I* didn't like!"

Inevitably there were repercussions. Marriage was a counter-revolutionary concept in the early seventies and Ellie had resorted to it purely for its weaponlike effect, knowing that her father took it seriously. By the time Ellie and Syed had escaped and struggled back to London in tortuous stages; initially on foot, then hitching a lift in a maniac's car, followed by bus, train - then foot again, Daphne's apparent fever-seizure prior to their frantic departure had not incapacitated her for long. She had managed by a roundabout route to get word of these fictitious marriage plans to Syed's father.

Syed looked pale and subdued after the inevitable paternal phone call.

"He insists that we visit him," he shrugged, "I can't refuse, your father is a *mouse* by comparison, as you'll very soon find out."

Already she deeply regretted her impulsive outburst.

Sadly almost the entire sum of money they had laboriously saved up and set aside for their journey east (a rites of passage trip virtually obligatory for anyone young and hip in those days, although Syed had understandable misgivings since eastern mysticism was coals to Newcastle for him, and he knew his long hair wouldn't go down well in home territory), now had to be channelled into this enforced journey to Stockholm, a thousand miles away in the wrong direction.

Long afterwards Ellie suspected that Syed might have intentionally scuppered their road trek east, for he suggested they buy their Volkswagen (the 'in' car for such journeys) in Munich, where it would be conveniently right hand drive *and* cheap. Well, it *was* right hand drive, and it might indeed have been cheap too - if only the Deutschmark had kept to the same conversion rate as the last time Syed bothered to check it out. As it was, the pound had nosed-dived to previously unchartered depths against it. All they could afford when they flew from Heathrow to Munich was a shaky old car that would struggle to even reach Stockholm.

Sure enough the engine developed a spasmodic hiccough about an hour north of Munich, whereupon Syed declared the best remedy was to floor the accelerator and drive at top speed to clear the blockage. All this achieved was the shedding of various loose bits of car: hubcaps, the exhaust tailpipe, rear door handles, bits of metal trim - that sort of thing. In a sense his remedy *did* work though; it may have failed to cure the hiccoughs but it eliminated the impression of shakiness because all the sources of rattling fell off. Unfortunately their exhilarating burst of speed caught them up with what must be the entire British army based in Germany, an unbelievably long convoy of army trucks and armoured tanks taking a lazy jaunt down the autobahn, called winter 'manoeuvres'.

Syed, having stayed in the fast lane and sailed past a good five miles of this column, suddenly decided he should 'rest' the car and dutifully tucked into the slow lane. It was unquestionably a mistake. Try driving a cheap, dilapidated old heap of a car suffering spasmodic hiccoughs whilst sandwiched between a lorryload of red faced, grinning soldiers clutching sniper rifles to the front of you, and a two stocky, beatle browed machine gunners practising homing in on their target (the back of your head) to your rear. Every time Syed signalled his urgent intention to move back out into the fast lane and escape this lethal trap they laughed with sadistic and no doubt racially spiced malice, whilst perilously narrowing the gap between the vehicles and gleefully waggling their guns at the nape of his neck.

Relief only came because twilight suddenly thickened and the pretty, early evening mist congealed into the sludgiest, densest peasouper fog Ellie had ever known, - and she had naturally known many from a childhood spent astride the banks of a meandering river in Kent.

At first it seemed to increase their danger, for shots fired blind into the deep swirling fog at an enemy car who had cheekily infiltrated their midst might not even trigger a military reprimand, let alone an official investigation; but suddenly, miraculously and without warning, the entire convoy peeled off sharp right down an exit slip road and vanished like ghostly spectres into the night. They were alone at last, on a fog shrouded motorway in the middle of nowhere.

Syed pulled into a lay-by and sorrowfully studied the car's decrepit condition. Important parts had fallen off or been prised off by the army nudging at their bumper. He decided that even if the car was still *just about* roadworthy it was madness to continue in such poor visibility. Unable to see the 'hand in front of one's face' sounds a clichéd exaggeration, but it was honestly true.

They slept fitfully on the rear seat cradled in each other's arms, deriving only the tiniest morsel of shared warmth and comfort in the icy dampness. Ellie was restlessly haunted by her father's jeering voice which kept repeating 'I told you so, told you so, so-so' all through the long, uncomfortable night.

In the morning they were still enveloped by fog, but gradually the swirling greyness thinned and lifted to reveal a beautiful world. A world drenched in rainbow droplets like prisms of coloured light where the horizontal rays of sunlight burned through the mist. It was a vision of such spectacular beauty that they could not be bothered to quarrel over who was most to blame for taking the wrong route, because they now discovered themselves nearly at Flensburg in the very centre of Jutland, whereas a long way back they should have remembered Denmark was not a solid block of land but broken into islands, and taken the easterly route to Puttgarden and the ferry.

It took the entire day to correct the mistake, so that by the time their gallant car stuttered into Puttgarden they just managed to catch the last ferry by a whisker. It deposited them in Rodbyhavn at midnight, and they soon found Rodbyhavn at midnight was not a pretty place. It was an industrial ghost town abandoned to drunks. Drunk pedestrians lurched along pavements wrapping themselves round lamp posts and vomiting into the gutter; drunk drivers criss-crossed the main road jumping red lights and climbing the pavements before overturning into roadside ditches; and mad drunk cyclists rode without lights on the wrong side of roads and fell off into the path of oncoming cars.

They badly needed somewhere warm to sleep after their cold, sleepless night in the car, but sadly all the welcoming hotels turned out to be brothels in disguise, while the hostile ones were manned exclusively by drunken bell hops who burped and pretended there were no rooms left - apart from the exorbitantly expensive master suites.

At last they found a dingy hotel near the port, where the night porter was just sober enough to sense he could pocket their room money if he gave them a double room on the condition they were out before seven in the morning when a 'really famous film star' would be booking in!

The drive through Sweden was one of restrained beauty. Ellie had expected frozen arctic wastes and foraging reindeer, but her latitude perspective was evidently wrong and they travelled smoothly east from Helsingborg to Stockholm without glimpsing the melted remains of a single snowflake. The sky was an unblemished pale ice blue, the patchy silvered branches of endless birch trees shimmered in the almost horizontal sunlight, and for once the road took them dead straight in the correct direction.

For much of the way it was peaceful. There was little traffic on the road and, fanciful though it sounds, Syed's alternation of crazy speeds and staid driving had indeed cured the respiratory/digestive problems of their car. Ellie thought it must have lain idle for months and needed to relearn how to circulate petrol and balance air, whereas Syed was convinced there were underlying emotional and psychological issues affecting its performance. He had apparently given it just the right amount of sympathy and encouragement, the ideal mix of stick and carrot.

They started by sharing the driving equally, taking two hour stints apiece, but gradually Syed claimed more and more of the driving on the grounds of this very special relationship he had with the car. He was convinced it purred when he drove it!

He still looked just as handsome and lived life with all his previous warmth, alertness and intelligence; but Ellie increasingly worried about two (until now dormant) character traits that their new round the clock co-existence was allowing to emerge. One was this insane *special relationship* he had with the car (tantamount to saying he was the better driver, or even the more sensitive human being), the second his almost pathological horror of being in the wrong. He would twist, bend and manipulate arguments into bizarre, contorted shapes in order to prove that he had not actually made a mistake, and if any mistake *had* been made it must of course be hers! Fortunately he could still be dispassionate about most topics *except* those related to the mechanics of travel: departure times, speed, distance, map reading, absorbing oral directions - that kind of thing, so Ellie was not forced to take the blame for everything and their other conversations were still just as pleasurably riveting as before.

It did make her worry about their projected journey east though. No way could she cheerfully shoulder the blame for travelling bungles for weeks on end. Perhaps this was his very intention - to cunningly and doubly ensure that they did not go.

As they finally neared Stockholm Syed turned noticeably subdued. It was as if they were entering the dark shadow-cloud of his father's influence, and his gloomy apprehension spread to Ellie.

"He'll manipulate you. Flatter you or ignore you, or both in turns. Most certainly he'll try to undermine me in your eyes, so you'll need to be ready for that."

"Sure," Ellie said nervously. "But he *won't* influence me. Haven't I just managed to shut the door on my own father due to his attitude to you?"

"But your father is mild and gentlemanly by comparison," Syed stared balefully at the ribbon of road ahead, "Mine is..."

For Syed to run out of words was an ominous sign indeed.

Finding his way through Stockholm in the dark of a cold January night, in a car that had misted up like a sauna, took all of Syed's concentration. Ellie was vaguely, eerily aware of passing between tall, ghostly, elegant façades of buildings, flickerings of street lights reflected in murky strips of water, and periodic jolts as their wheels ran over the tramcar rails. She could tell from his silent, set profile that he had no feelings of pleasant anticipation, only a deep seated dread. At last he parked in a tree lined road on the crest of a hill, where he sat motionless for a period of silent meditation. Then together they walked reluctantly down the path towards a large secluded house set in a tousled woodland garden, where the only vocal welcome was excited high pitched yapping. The door half-opened and a liver coloured dachshund slithered out and scurried towards them, yapping, wriggling and squirming. It threw itself at Syed's legs, peeing with excitement all over his shoes.

"He must have recognised me," he said ruefully.

In sharp contrast it treated Ellie to a vicious nip in the ankle, which she took as an accurate transmission of its owners' attitude, namely that she was an unwelcome outsider with no business there at all.

Although the delirious volley of barking must surely have alerted the entire household of their arrival, no-one came to the door. Eventually a servant sheepishly let them in, then disappeared muttering something Ellie couldn't understand. She supposed this was a parallel take on Syed's experience of her father turning his back on the offered handshake, but for Syed it was a double rejection, as this was his own family. Or not entirely - not in the sense of a blood relationship, for he too had a stepmother. He also had cute little twin half-sisters because Ellie had seen their photographs, but they would already be fast asleep in bed, seeing as they were only six years old and it was now past ten o'clock at night.

It suddenly seemed as if they had driven an awful long way to be given the cold shoulder.

At last, footsteps approached and Elaine, Syed's stepmother, appeared in the living room doorway, silhouetted against the twinkling lights from a tall Christmas tree and the more grandiose lozenges of an imposing chandelier. She looked strained and apprehensive, but she gave Syed a welcoming peck on the cheek and graciously invited them in, vaguely including Ellie in this directive.

> "We're in a bit of chaos at the moment," she at last smiled with genuine amusement, "that rat Ehsan-ul-Haque just decamped to the Bangladeshi embassy with most of the official silver. He'd been eyeing it all along - I guess it's a fair cut in some ways. At least we've still got the plates to eat off!"

Syed smiled knowingly, and Ellie felt inexplicably shy because she knew such a tiny fraction of his life, an intensity of knowledge perhaps but concentrated into a mere five months, whereas this tall, handsome woman from New Zealand could comfortably allude to people, places, politics and shared experiences about which she was utterly ignorant.

When offered the chance to 'freshen up' in her bedroom upstairs, fear gnawed at her again when she saw the narrow single bed, puritanical as a nun's, and faced the realisation that the comfort and pleasure of sleeping with Syed was a thing strictly forbidden her in this house. Despite all the ways in which Syed had tried to prepare her to be strong she felt suddenly weak - as if she had lost the battle already. They would unite against her; she who was frivolous, blond and privileged. And because she had stupidly mentioned the marriage word, they doubtless adjudged her a schemer, a predator. She felt not only alone and misunderstood, but also powerless to correct the image they had of her because she had somehow surrendered her identity the moment she entered their house. She had even lost confidence in Syed's love. If he really loved her he wouldn't have brought her here to be hated.

She splashed cold water on her pale, stricken face, then, a ghostlike shadow of her former self, reluctantly descended the stairs.

As if seated on a resplendent throne his father had full occupation of the main sofa in the living room, wrapped in a peacock blue and violet silk dressing gown to plainly demonstrate that their late arrival had disturbed his routine of early to bed. He stared at Ellie with a mixture of appraisal, appreciation and contempt. She could not tell which held dominance - except that past experience of older men with his fleshy look of unrestrained self-indulgence suggested the appreciation was for her body, while the contempt extended to her mind, soul and race. His eyes eventually slid off her towards a squat chair, and she assumed this was an invitation to sit on it.

"Your father telephoned me," he announced. His voice relished authority but unlike Syed's was heavily accented. Then he sipped at a tall tumbler of whisky before adding - almost as an afterthought, "His message is: he will disinherit you if you insist on marrying Syed." He gave her a knowing look, "I'm sure you don't want that."

Ellie was momentarily lost for words, but eventually mumbled a preference for love over money, which in turn roused his sincere disgust.

"Syed has equally stupid notions. *More* stupid when you consider he is neither blond, blue-eyed nor the holder of a British passport."

Syed came in at this juncture, having obviously made a supreme effort to brush and tame his long hair so as to minimize his father's abhorrence of it. Ellie later learnt that he had been allotted an even harder, narrower single bed like a monk's pallet in a tiny cupboard of a room about a quarter the size of hers, to teach him humility.

She concentrated on trying not to see either herself or Syed through his father's eyes; tried to cling to her image of them in their own context. Young students, full of fresh optimism, carefree and free. And she reminded herself of Syed's warning, "He'll undermine me in your eyes."

She *could* understand something of the rage and frustration they must arouse in their parents'generation. Having bravely fought through the horrors of one - or even two - world wars with so much suffering and deprivation, it must be exasperating to contend with her generation blithely ignoring or condemning all they had fought for. Her contempories, the 'hippie' generation, cheerfully derided money, power, capitalism, nerdy ambition, work, marriage and family values. They declared that love, peace and happiness (and admittedly a few drugs on the side) were all they needed in life, and they prided themselves they had orchestrated a whole new 'social revolution'. But *had* they? She sighed. Whether or not they effectively had, there was no need for Syed's father to be so out and out condemnatory. *Now* she could understand why Syed had busily nurtured his obsession for being right - it was a necessary shield against his father's constant bombardment.

"Sit down!" his father bellowed. Then, lowering his voice lest it carry into the next room where Elaine was hovering, he confided proudly, "Plenty of exceptional beauties wanted to marry *me*, but *I* opted instead for a woman with common sense." He glared at Ellie for her empty airheadedness before adding, a shade doubtfully, "I have never *once* regretted it."

"As you know, I always try to follow your example."

His father glanced furiously at him, remembering anew why he resented this mocking, glib-tongued, self-contained son who rationed his respect and refused to acknowledge the immensity of the debt he owed his father. He would be nowhere and nothing without him. Why, from the initial intervention of his sperm determining both conception *and* gender, through to the fact that his glitteringly illustrious career had provided Syed with a decent education and access to a prominent University, all was *his,* not Syed's, doing. And how did Syed show gratitude for being the eldest son with an international upbringing and decent prospects? With not one iota of real respect, that's how! By self-indulgent vanity, growing his hair like a girl's, wearing ridiculous clothes and *dancing*!

He felt so upset by Syed's outrageous appearance and immature espousal of dance and music as a serious form of culture (mere superficiality, light entertainment, career options for those without a brain) that he was tempted to bellow aloud his grief and anger. However he must *not* give Syed the satisfaction of knowing how upset he felt. Instead he created a diversionary noise with crushed ice, tongs and a whisky decanter before continuing.

"My advice is NOT to get married," he announced, certain Syed would not have anticipated this position.

"I have absolutely no intention of marrying," Syed assured him, truthfully enough.

His father gave a deep sigh and heaved himself off the sofa, still nursing the whisky. He strode out of the room without a backward glance. When he had gone Syed shrugged resignedly and sighed. Sighing seemed to be *the* eloquent language of this house.

As Ellie lay drifting into solitary sleep between the cold sheets of her lonely bed she wondered if Syed's father hated her more because she belonged to the stock of colonisers: an arrogant, imperious, slow-witted, lazy and pampered people; or because of *who* she was as an individual: the spoilt daughter of an English snob with upperclass pretensions. Once she had realised they were really one and the same, she fell to wondering if he didn't simply hate her because she was young and with Syed; but she knew of course really that it was all of them. When she eventually fell asleep she was *still* wondering whether, even if she hadn't been any of those things, he would still hate her. Determinedly she shut her mind to him, only for him to surreptitiously invade her dreams in a dazzlingly bright peacock silk robe and dark glasses, wielding a sharp bladed axe with which he crushed slithers of ice cubes into an ice bucket of whisky, mouthing 'Syed hates you too!'

There were occasional pleasant moments. The little twins were adorable and worshipped Syed, although she could imagine that would all be fervently drummed out of them before they reached the danger age of twelve or thirteen and his malign influence might pervert them. The dog stopped nipping at her ankles and peed less frequently on Syed's shoes, then on their fifth day they were allowed a door key so that they could come and go a little more freely. Syed's father had by now given up trying to influence or argue with Syed and merely ignored him. At mealtimes he concentrated on food, and conversation was strictly limited to day to day political or social issues that were directed solely at Elaine but meant to impress and be overheard by everyone present.

On the sixth day he *at last* asked Syed, "When, exactly, are you leaving?"

Syed had been waiting for this. "Tomorrow," he answered, feigning deep regret, and Ellie quietly crossed her fingers.

As they drove inexorably westwards with the low sun lighting their backs and tall pine trees lining the horizon, Ellie could sense Syed relaxing and her old self returning, yet she had an uneasy feeling she had left something precious behind. Not a triviality like sunglasses, warm gloves or a scarf, the usual casualties of such visits, but something more personal, more vital. Perhaps it was her self-confidence, or what she assumed was her personality, or even her supposed intelligence. Or was it simply the innocent quality of her love for Syed, and his for her?

"*Why* was so much fuss made about the stolen silver? Surely it's hardly your father's fault Bangladesh came into being?" she asked suddenly.

"No. But it's the ideal pretext for Pakistani diplomats to steal government possessions and blame it on the Bangladeshis. Those who don't like my father - and believe me there are plenty of them - will leap at this chance to insinuate *he* was the real thief."

"Ah," said Ellie. Then, after a pause, "Do you despise me for being so slow and English?"

Syed grinned, "Only for being English. I like you being slow."

"The only reason I'll admit *you're* clever," she said frowning, "is because I now don't want to drive east anymore. Behind the steering wheel of a car you become unbelievably horrible."

"Perhaps it's only then that my true self emerges."

That night they reached Copenhagen. Much to Ellie's surprise and delight the room Syed's father had insisted on booking for them proved to be an enormous double room romantically overlooking the sea.

"*Why on earth* has he permitted us to sleep together now, after all that effort to separate us?"

"What my father most hates, apart from being wrong or being *liked*, is being predictable," and for one awful moment before throwing off his clothes Syed looked to Ellie almost the spitting image of his father - but of course a more handsome version without any of the excess flesh or age.

"Plus it's by far the most expensive suite. So he'll relish the thought of our embarrassment when we have to pay for it, which, *if* we even can, will leave us no money at all for the rest of our journey."

Syed smiled ruefully so that the fleeting resemblance mercifully vanished, and she saw him as his loveable self once again.

Old Friends

Daylight was fading and the valleys had dissolved into pools of mist and dark shadow. But instead of appreciating their mysterious beauty, we regretted that London was still so far away. We should have been there by now, but having agreed to take *yet another* deviation to see *yet another* windswept longbarrow, we were still struggling along a tortuous minor road, somewhere in the middle of Wiltshire.

Or was that last mound a tumulus, not a longbarrow? Not that it mattered - I had honestly ceased to care whether I recognised anything correctly, after what had been (even *before* getting lost) a mind-numbingly long day traipsing dutifully after ancient legends. It felt as if the evening mist had literally invaded our eyesight for nothing looked clear anymore; maybe we had stared too long at those curious circles of giant stones or the mysterious mounds of earth (could Camelot *really* lie beneath that muddy hill?), puzzling over the half-truths, part-fantasies of history.

This trip was our attempt to satisfy the romantic yearnings of Rupert, who was nearly twelve and had fallen under the spell of ancient myths and folklore. But the rest of us failed to share his enthralment. One reason being that I had carelessly forgotten to bring anything waterproof so the fierce driving rain had chilled us to the bone. And the other that Sarah, who was nine, was now so thickly plastered in a glutinous layer of mud after sliding down Glastonbury Tor that she had become glued to the back seat of the car.

Hugo peered morosely ahead at the road which snaked and vanished into the twilight, dismally computing the miles still to be driven. Immediately, as if attuned to his thoughts, the car gave a cough, then an ominous, choking stutter. In the uneasy silence that followed I could distinctly sense that all of a sudden he held me chiefly to blame for this foolhardy expedition, although I knew that I had definitely tried to argue Rupert out of his obsession just as much as he had.

"We'll never make it back tonight," he predicted grimly, "the car's decided."

My eyes raked the rolling hills for signs of habitation, a welcoming light or some spark of comfort, but there was only emptiness. The road looked even narrower than it had before dusk fell, owing to our solitary headlight (at least mercifully working, though only with a feeble, sickly glare). Fortunately it had just enough power to illuminate the sign at the next T junction. I had been willing it to say LONDON 15 miles, although that was pure wishful thinking, - it in fact said DEVIZES 3 miles. The name immediately struck a dimly remembered chord.

"Stop!" I yelled, noticing a dilapidated public phone booth propped against the rear wall of the pub we encountered round the next bend. "There just *might* be somewhere we could stay!"

(I should perhaps explain that these events I am describing took place in 1985, so phoning was not the simple matter of tapping out a number on a mobile that it is now).

Hugo kept the engine running while I scrambled out and hurriedly trod down the brambles barricading the phone booth door. It seemed unlikely there would be an instrument in there, let alone an actual line connection, since it had obviously not been used in years. Hugo must have feared the car would refuse to restart if he switched off the engine; and he must have reckoned I had gone mad and was booking dinner for four at King Arthur's round table the way he looked at me as I struggled to dial with my numbed fingers, having made the miraculous discovery that the instrument *was* working after all.

In actual fact my mind had not run amok; it had simply remembered my connection to Devizes. I had once visited a grey stone house on the banks of a disused canal near there, shortly before my fourteenth birthday. My parents were cruising in and out of Norwegian fjords at the time and I had been sent to stay with a school friend called Alice. Her parents in turn offloaded us onto her aunt who lived in this house called Lock Keeper's Lodge. It was a strange name because the canal ran level for miles in either direction so there *was* no lock, and presumably never had been, even when the canal was a busy highway.

Alice's uncle was a canal fanatic, madder than a March hare. He worked round the clock every weekend shovelling out tons of silted mud and forests of weeds that clogged what had once been an important waterway (as he never tired of telling us). He had devoted ten entire years of weekends to restoring a mere half mile of canal to perfect mint condition, and he used to whistle merry but mischievous nautical songs as he sailed his barge called 'Alice in Wonderland' (in honour of Alice, I think, not Lewis Carroll) up and down it.

I was acting on the hunch they *might* still be living there. The uncle had been so besotted with canals it was difficult to imagine he would move away, and there had been enough mud still to be scooped out to last him several lifetimes. Directory enquiries as good as confirmed they were there, since their surname still matched the address.

"Hello!" I yelled in excitement when someone picked up the phone.

Then I made an effort to rein in my exuberance. She might not remember me. Or she might be angry that I had subsequently abandoned Alice as a friend. That was how Alice might see it but I felt we had simply gone our own ways. As happens when you grow up, and different relationships with two different men draw you apart. Or she might be remembering that Uncle Rob (her husband) was a bit too interested in young teenage girls, in the way some uncles are, and still be nursing her resentment.

When I patiently explained exactly who I was, with dates and names to confirm it, she sounded quite pleased and did not hesitate to invite us over for tea. I of course cunningly glossed over the tricky predicament of a car on its last legs; exhausted, sleepy and hungry children smothered in mud; and a stressed husband fed up with ruins and just bursting to tell me 'I told you so'. After all, a foot in the door was all that was needed initially. Greater hospitality would then most likely ensue; barren couples turn broody over endearing children, I did remember that about them. Although the Uncle Rob's drooling was admittedly a little different.

"They used to have a couple of old fashioned covered wagons on wheels," I told Hugo. "They were once shepherd's huts, used at lambing time. I'm sure she wouldn't mind us staying one night in them - they had narrow beds but nice warm blankets."

The car managed to keep going despite frequent bouts of coughing, but we almost missed the driveway entrance because it was on the wrong side of the road, the blind side without any operational headlight. Collectively we breathed a sigh of relief when Hugo finally switched off the labouring engine and a blissful silence ensued. The lights shone cheerfully out from the downstairs rooms, but no-one came to greet us.

Feeling a little wrong footed I walked hesitantly to the door and knocked; loudly but not thunderously, in case they were deaf but not wanting to seem pushy and rude. I could hear the approaching click of a metal tipped walking stick and the shuffle of bedroom slippers. It was only then that I realised how long twenty years was for people already past their prime. Her voice had sounded strong enough on the phone, but then she always did have a megaphone-type voice, a harsh, barking orders way of speaking without any soft soothing tones, perhaps because she had never cooed to any baby or bothered to whisper sweet nothings to Uncle Rob. Which was possibly why he took to drooling over Alice and me, (and others no doubt, if ever he got the chance).

Wheezy breathing and muffled grunts accompanied the dragging back of bolts, whereupon the door creaked open to reveal an astonishingly white haired old lady, the white wispy strands responding to some hidden electrical charge and standing upright like dandelion fluff.

I guessed she must be in her mid seventies. She was wearing a tartan woollen shawl, a tweed skirt, incongruously bright pink woolly bedsocks and bedroom slippers that were probably made of sealskin but looked like a couple of downtrodden dogs. I tried to tear my eyes away from these bizarre slippers - once I realised they weren't a couple of real living dachshunds - and politely meet her eyes. They stared back at me unblinkingly and were the only feature (apart from the telephone voice) that had not changed or aged at all; cold, piercing, ice-blue eyes. I remembered them with a sudden feeling of unease; eyes sharp as knives and as cruelly critical, especially after they had noted the amount of mud Uncle Rob collected on the soles of his shoes and wiped off on her inherited Persian runner, or the length of leg Alice liked to expose on a carefree summer's day.

"Who the hell are *you*?" she demanded sharply. "I *never* receive visitors after dark."

"I spoke with you on the phone only five minutes ago." I tried to be very calm and patient, and not at all indignant. Old people can be forgetful, I reminded myself. "You invited me over. I'm Chloe - I stayed here with you twenty years ago."

"Ah," she sighed, "*how* we grow old..." Then her eyes snapped back into focus as she examined my face and body with a puzzled frown. "Were you *always* this much younger than me?"

"I'm Alice's age," I explained politely, "And I always have been."

"*Thank God* you weren't a friend of mine!" she declared. And I hoped her relief was because I did not show her up as having aged at a far more accelerated rate than me, rather than because if she ever had me as a friend it smacked of appalling judgment.

In retrospect it would have been wiser to have driven off there and then. Age had not remotely mellowed her and even that brief exchange told me she had metamorphosed into a thoroughly mad old bat. But the crippled condition of the car clouded my thinking. There was no sign of Uncle Rob so I assumed he must have died, and I certainly did not want to mention him in case it reminded her of the drooling and turned her even nastier.

"She's got a few screws loose," was all I warned Hugo and the kids in a tactful whisper when I reported back to them, "but I'm sure she's harmless. She says to come in," I added, although truthfully she had said nothing of the sort.

We trooped in, the kids' normal exuberance thankfully subdued by the twenty to thirty miles we had walked whilst circumnavigating the outer rings of hill forts or holy shrines, beacons or burial grounds - whatever they once were. Hugo, I could tell, was teased by curiosity, at the same time as suffering more than any of us from the strain of the sick car. He always said the only reason he wished we had a little more money and could replace it, was because he felt so drained from keeping it running through sheer will power.

"Hello Alice, long time no see," said Aunt Trudy with much less frostiness than before. She had noticed with relief that Sarah's thighs were at least properly covered, even if it was with her old enemy - sticky lumps of mud.

I had the wit to realise her craziness in confusing Sarah with Alice would fortunately serve to increase our welcome, even if entailed me being mistaken for Alice's mum (who was her younger sister - but would be sixty something by now!)

"I hope you're not expecting to be paid for that shoddy piece of work on the veranda," she suddenly addressed Hugo haughtily, "because I shan't give you another penny."

"Oh no," he sounded charmingly reassuring, "It was a gift, and my pleasure."

He had a natural knack with old ladies owing to prior experience of senile dementia. His favourite grandmama had irretrievably lost her marbles near the end and he was the only one of her grandchildren, in fact *the* only other person, who managed to enter and share her alternative world. In the normal run of things he would not have taken kindly to being mistaken for a cowboy builder, not being keen on DIY or even remotely practical, plus he proudly imagined that he looked what he actually was: a talented, dedicated, but much too sensitive artist.

I politely offered to help with the tea and discovered that although her eyes might *look* sharp they were alarmingly blind to a great many fundamental things. Such as where she last put the biscuit tin, which position turned the electric kettle 'on', the difference between tea leaves and coffee grounds, and how to tell when an onion had truly rotted. Interspersed with wiping grime from long forgotten tea cups or hunting for the tray - and eventually finding it plugging the draught where a window pane had broken, I surreptitiously weeded out the worst of the rotting vegetables from their rack, amazed that her sense of smell had not detected the sizeable pool of green slime oozing from a sack of putrefying potatoes. I fancied grimly that I could detect signs of genuine pond life gyrating about in its dark green depths; frogs' spawn, minnows and miniature water snakes, while dozens of happy-go-lucky water boatmen played leapfrog across its scummy surface.

Venturing further I found that mould and mushrooms had taken full mastery of the larder walls, and something extremely sour was dripping frothily from an old cracked jug. I began to feel queasy and wondered anxiously whether we had enough picnic sandwiches left to stretch to something of a supper. Her stomach had doubtless grown a tough leather lining by now, but someone as young as Sarah could much more easily be poisoned. Then, while she still continued to hunt for the biscuit tin in ever widening circles, I snatched my opportunity to wash the cups, plates and cutlery, and to swill off the more revolting kitchen surfaces with a powerful dose of disinfectant.

Whilst I was urgently scrubbing away I tried hard to keep the lid fastened on my imagination, for the panoply of different vile smells suggested death and decay of the animal as well as vegetable kingdom. I had no desire to find a dead cat in the broom cupboard or – worse still, yet my nostrils quivered at the pungent possibility - a dead dog in the old, no longer functioning slow oven of the Aga. I even began to wonder nervously if she might not have hung Uncle Rob up the chimney to smoke like an old ham. Those inquisitors of late medieval times would have burnt her at the stake without a second thought, I decided, since her spice rack and shelves provided more evidence of witchcraft than witch-haters usually bothered to obtain.

"Sugar in your tea?" she asked Rupert.

I signalled frantically for him to decline. I was fairly convinced that whatever congealed granules were sulking in that bowl they were definitely not sugar!

But I had to conceal my apprehension as he took the offered biscuit, which was doubtless home to a community of weevils, aware that I could not prevent all offered morsels passing our lips or she would notice and take offence.

"How about you, Headman?" she enquired snootily of Hugo, but without the full-blown snobbery you would expect someone like her to use on a native tribal chief.

Hugo was French but had long been exposed to the English island mentality - which he claimed was anti-French above all else. He had his own subtle ways of dealing with perceived racist slights but he merely gave her another of his charming smiles, so I guessed he was reckoning the engine needed the entire night to relax and cool down. Or it was because of his natural reverence for old age, or that she reminded him fondly of his grandmère.

The hot tea soon loosened her tongue. Maybe she had not talked for many years - or to no-one except herself. She did not listen though; neither to what she herself said nor to anyone else, so that although Rupert patiently told her his name at least ten times she always forgot it two seconds later. In the end he gave up and told her a different name each time, which he thoroughly enjoyed and she thankfully failed to notice. Sarah was not even asked her name because she was mostly Alice, but sometimes Chloe (which should have been me!), while Hugo was either Headman or Howard. She pronounced the name 'Howard' with such a lilting softness that I began to wonder whether he was her real true love, but something went tragically wrong and she married Rob on the rebound.

"*I'd* have liked a pretty girl like you," she told Sarah (or Alice) "only we couldn't have children. Or *Rob* couldn't.'"

That took me by surprise. I always assumed their childlessness was her preference; that she deliberately chose to keep a clean house and avoid the mess of babies. Could his drooling have been a vestigial reflex then, like an amputee still feeling the pain in his missing leg? Perhaps I got everything back to front in those days, in the dizzy foolishness of being merely fourteen.

"You oughtn't to be leading Alice astray," she suddenly stared at me accusingly, "skinny dipping in the canal, down by the weeping willow. Don't think I didn't see you. Cheeky hussy."

I could remember us swinging from the overhanging branches of the willow and dropping into the water with a violent splash - so violent that Uncle Rob complained we would empty the canal if we were not more careful. I was sure we were never naked though, we would never have dared to be, certainly not when so close to their house. It was probably just Alice's bare legs she was still fretting over…

"You *must* stay for supper," she declared forcefully, "you can't drive round here in the blackout. I've got some emergency rations we can tuck into."

She then led me off to inspect her ration cupboard, which was next to the broom cupboard under the stairs. It was relatively dry and benign smelling, so I hoped this was where she had finally located the biscuit tin, rather than in some of the less savoury locations she had searched through. Sure enough there were stacks of tins and bottles: pilchards, sardines, corned beef, jellied ham, spaghetti hoops, ambrosia creamed rice, peach slices in syrup and all the other delicacies of wartime stockpiles.

Thank goodness they never stamped them with '*Best before*' dates in that long ago era, since that would confirm we were more than forty years too late! I had a lurking fear that tinned food might prove *even more* dangerous than rotting 'fresh food', since the chemical preservatives might have reacted with the tin and produced some fatal form of lead poisoning, but I did not dare say a word. I had now become her sister Violet, you see, the one who was Alice's mother. She giggled gleefully at our conspiratorial cheek in raiding our parents' goodies, and I did not have the heart to break the spell. I guess I was enjoying the feeling of genuinely being liked instead of hated for a brief moment or two.

I did wonder if it *was* the right tactic - to humour her, to willingly enter her fantasy world. Should I not steer her back to present realities, gently remind her that she was an elderly lady living on her own, that Rob was no longer around, and Howard even less so, and that she really needed a live-in companion who would help her keep the house clean?

Suddenly I felt a deep shame for the way Alice and I used to giggle over her primness and dirt phobia, despising her for her obsessive mopping and re-mopping of floors. We saw her then from our very limited perspective: a crabby woman, fifty and therefore utterly ancient, bizarrely preferring a bottle of Jeyes fluid to a decent wine or even her husband, as drab and passionless as it was possible to be. It never remotely occurred to us that she might have once been a happy, normal teenager just like us, romping around with her younger sister, blushing and lusting after Howard, then longing for children with Rob. She had probably channelled her domestic urges into an all-out war on dirt only when the hope of children faded for ever.

It seemed strangely ironic that now, after all those years being a cleanliness addict, she had ultimately found release through living in utter filth and squalor. Could the volte face be deliberate? Or had she simply grown oblivious to her surroundings?

The house had now grown more fertile than the weed choked garden. Strange growths sprung from wicker baskets; moss, lichen and fungi smothered the roof tiles; assorted liquids fermented in buckets and rain butts, busily oozing and bubbling. In fact the entire structure of the house seemed suspect. The once sturdy stone walls had bowed inwards and were eroding at their base, the old oak beams had shed little conical piles of powder - like a line of sand dunes - from the endless gnawing of woodworm, and all in all it would not be long before it could be passed off as an ancient pre-Saxon ruin.

If the night were not so dark I might have been tempted to inspect the canal, for in the general spirit of reversals I half-expected to find it bone dry, meticulously neat, and just as wonderfully polished as her house once was!

It was not safe for her to live alone though, not anymore. Quite apart from the physical problems, her mind was not anchored to reality. At any moment she might use rat poison in place of cornflour, set the house on fire due to its dodgy wiring, or fall down the stairs and not be found for months or even years. I ought to find out where Alice lives, I decided, let her know about her aunt's state...

"Could you be a dear and go get the eggs, Alice?" she asked Sarah, who was busily inspecting the interesting way the mud on her jeans was drying and cracking into jigsaw-like patterns. "Don't go worrying about that mud. We're in the country here."

"What eggs?" Sarah asked with a puzzled little frown.

"My eggs, of course!" she gave a mad cackle. "I suppose you thought I was infertile, eh? Everybody else bloody did. And naturally *Rob* encouraged that all he could."

"I'll help you get them," Hugo could see Sarah was floundering, unused to the vagaries of old age and bewildered by the strange bitterness of her comments.

They duly found a flock of chickens roosting quietly in the shepherd's wagon, the one I had originally proposed for our sleeping quarters. They apparently looked quite healthy, with bright pink combs, beady eyes and glossy feathers. They had cunningly devised their own system of eluding foxes by enjoying free range foraging during daylight hours, then retreating into the wagon at night via a small window propped open on a catch, leaving an opening too small and awkward for any fox to steal through.

They squawked loudly when Hugo shone the car torch at their perches, but allowed eight eggs to be removed without a single peck of protest. Hugo, being French and therefore imaginative about omelettes, was eagle eyed enough to discover healthy clumps of dandelion leaves and borage on his way back to the house. Thus our supper fell into place without undue risk of poisoning or any need to open a rusty wartime tin, and therefore be forced to hear nasty jibes about wicked French collaborators and how much too easily the French Government had surrendered. Hugo became unhappy with that sort of talk, and perhaps she realised this because she had *at last* understood he was neither a builder nor a 'Headman', but French.

All five of us became French over supper, as a matter of fact. It transpired she spoke the language well, having done a year's course at the Sorbonne long ago when she was only eighteen and still hopeful of ensnaring Howard. Her mind wandered delightedly back to the cobbled alleyways of the Quartier Latin with its bookshops, watchmakers' dens, pavement cafés and boulangeries with fresh warm bakery smells. She became more than mildly coquettish with Hugo, and embarrassingly flirtatious with Rupert who was most confused by his precocious new role. This because she had overdone it with the mature bottle of claret she found tucked under the arm of the sofa, and had to be carried up the stairs to sleep it off by Hugo and me.

"Where shall *we* sleep?" Hugo wondered. "Now that the chickens have appropriated your shepherds' wagons."

"*Both* of them?"

"Well, the other's…even *less* habitable."

After witnessing the state of the kitchen and larder I could guess what he meant. Being made of wood those wagons would be vulnerable and I soon fancied I could hear - above the regular snores from upstairs - the sharp clicking of stag beetles and the scratching of rats, and an occasional sharp hoot of a hunting owl coming from their direction.

I shivered, once more wondering how and when uncle Rob had died. She seemed to have no fond memories of him. How could she have lived with him for more than forty years if all she felt was bitterness and disappointment? I found myself wondering whose obsession had come first: his with mud or hers with cleanliness. When she said snappily, whilst we were alone in the kitchen "Him and his wretched mud - well he's buried under it now, so he shouldn't complain," I had a terrible - but mercifully fleeting - vision of his body lying in the muddy underbelly of the canal. Had he slipped in? Or been pushed? I had had to shake off these gruesome imaginings and tell myself to get a grip; *of course* she must have meant buried in the churchyard, properly, in a grave, mud being just another word for earth.

We slept fitfully but surprisingly comfortably on a careful construction of sofa and armchair cushions, laid out like a giant mattress on the living room floor. We kept warm by skilfully overlapping the sections of rugs that had been ignored by the moths, although the stench of mothballs was nearly overpowering.

Our only moment of serious alarm was in the pearl grey light of early morning, when Aunt Trudy tottered down the stairs in a savagely motheaten dressing gown to make herself a cup of tea. The night had swept her memory clean of all happenings on the previous day, so imagine her horror - a mixture of anger and fear - on finding her house had been invaded by a family of total strangers! It was a blessed stroke of luck that Uncle Rob's shotgun was empty of cartridges, but Hugo did not know this vital, comforting detail when he opened his eyes to find the barrel aimed straight up his nostrils. It was only when Rupert had the presence of mind to try reasoning with her in French that she began to remember the previous evening, and a long two minutes before she finally laid down the gun and picked up the tea caddie.

"What's your favourite breakfast, then?" she asked Rupert. "Poached, fried, coddled, boiled or scrambled eggs?"

There was an awkward silence before Rupert mumbled, "Didn't we already *have* eggs for supper?" Then he must have remembered his manners as a guest, for he added, "Toast on its own's fine for me."

She grunted, "But we've got no bread… Tell you what though, I'll whip off and buy some."

I was lying beside Hugo, still rattled after his extremely near miss with the gun and too nervous to slip out from beneath the covers in my underwear to rescue my clothes from behind the sofa. For, now that guns had entered the equation, I had no wish to resurrect Aunt Trudy's fictional incident of Alice and me splashing naked in the canal and make her angry again - just when she seemed to be settling down. So I stayed feebly in the background whilst Rupert chatted to Trudy in the kitchen, guiltily aware that as a responsible mother *I* ought to be the one supervising breakfast. I could even have rustled up some recycled bread from yesterdays' sandwiches, if I had had the intelligence to think of it - and the diligence to scrape off the fillings. But I didn't.

They were speaking French again, arguing affably about the relative merits of croissants and pains au chocolat. Then I heard the door slam, a muffled "Au revoir cheri," and I remember feeling relieved that Rupert had obviously not gone with her.

Later he told me that he watched her from the kitchen window, which was mainly plugged by a plastic tray but still had a few panes of glass intact. These were thickly smeared with grime and hung with cobwebs, so allowed only a vague visibility of the outside world. It was therefore in an indistinct, blurred fashion that he saw her making determinedly for the dark arched shape of the canal bridge, where a couple of five barred gates prevented sheep from two rival farmers' herds mingling and muddling together.

She appeared to be brandishing an enormously long pole, and Rupert worried that she might be planning to batter some poor, defenceless sheep to death. It was a plausible suspicion for mutton chops and devilled sheep's kidneys might make a welcome break from endless eggs, and she had muttered 'mint sauce' when he mentioned he could detect the smell of mint from somewhere in the overgrown wilderness of her garden.

At this point he was distracted from his surveillance by some indoor action. A spider belayed to a screw on the window hinge was abseiling down to capture a bluebottle, so momentarily he forgot Trudy. Then he thought he saw her below the arch of the bridge. She appeared to be walking Christ-like upon the waters of the canal with only her upper body visible, the rest hidden behind the forest of weeds lining the bank. She was also going backwards, jabbing and poking at something with a pole, something pursuing her...

If he had only been aware that Uncle Rob's old canal boat, 'Alice in Wonderland', had been moored to the bridge, and she had untied it from its mooring after years of neglect, he *might* have interpreted these bizarre images correctly and recognised that she was punting the boat along the canal. But even if he *had* realised, he still might not have anticipated the danger.

The boat had spent nine years submerged, lightly beached on a cushion of mud, stranded more than actually afloat. It was in fact surprising she had enough strength in her arms to push it free of its muddy mooring. Nine years embedded in mud had not preserved its timbered hull, thus the moment it scraped clear of the mudshelf water began to seep in.

Rupert *did* notice she was sinking. Whereas at first she was visible from the waist upwards, soon just the top of her head could be seen, then that too disappeared.

At this point he yelled, "Help!" and rushed out to the garden. He assumed she was jabbing the sheep with her lance and had tripped on a tussock - due to walking backwards, and was now being trampled by the enraged flock. It took him more valuable seconds to readjust from this warped interpretation to the reality of the situation, but once he did, he again hollered "Help!" at a volume that spoke of real panic.

Both Hugo and I sprung to our feet and nearly collided in the doorway. Still pushing arms and legs into flapping clothing we sped down the path to the canal, just in time to witness the peaked roof surmounting the cramped cabin sink beneath the swirling surface of the water. More valuable seconds were wasted before we grasped exactly what had happened, for Rupert was incoherent in his distress. When we finally understood that Trudy had been *on* the boat we stared hopelessly at the churning water, so thickly muddied that you could see nothing of its depths. Its dark brown glassy surface stared maliciously back, suddenly flecked by tiny bubbles of creamy scum escaping upwards. They were doubtless the product of some pressurized release or an airlock in the cabin, but in my horror I imagined them coming from Trudy's gasping, frantic, desperately drowning lungs.

My brain worked sluggishly, as if it were as clouded as the silted water, which I willed to miraculously clear so that we could simply reach down a helping hand to fish her out. One is *supposed* to think and react at heightened speed in an emergency, but I remained rooted to the spot. Somewhere in the back of my mind, I knew that had the victim overboard been Rupert, Sarah or Hugo, or someone I *truly* loved, I would have instantly risked life and limb to dive in after them.

Instead I shivered violently from the sudden, irrational fear that it was a trick to get the better of me at last; if I were to enter the water in pursuit she would immediately fasten bony hands around my body and pull me down... It was a despicable thought but it gripped hold of me - just like her imaginary fingers - and I was powerless to shake it off.

In the vital seconds that I struggled with this stupidity Hugo, without any hesitation, plunged into the water and dived under. When he did not resurface my heart pounded and *at last* my brain cleared. She had grabbed *him* instead of me! Or he had banged his head on the deck of the boat, or got snarled up in the mooring rope, or, unable to see through the muddy water, had swum into the cabin and was trapped there, unable to find the way out...

Whilst Rupert futilely dangled a length of rope into the water I tried frantically to remember the geography of this section of canal. It was wider, deeper than the straight stretch of waterway to either side, and formed a sizeable basin where, in its working days, half a dozen boats could be tied up while their owners exchanged news or money with the lock keeper of Lock Keeper's Lodge. Perhaps it was deep because there really *had* been a lock there after all, only later they compensated for the difference in level by other means - maybe a gentle downhill slope imperceptible to the human eye. I thought there was a ladder built from wooden struts bolted into sheet metal to the left of the bridge, from long ago when I visited with Alice, but either it had rotted or the top rung was now underwater, for there was no sign of it.

"Rupert!" my voice shook, "Go dial 999. The phone's on the kitchen shelf!"

Hugo surfaced just at that moment, but I gestured to Rupert - who had turned back in relief - to still make the call. Hugo was at the limit of his breath, he must have been underwater for more than two minutes, meaning Trudy would have been under for more than three. She could not possibly still be breathing; not unless she had found some miracle pocket of air. I had proved myself ineffective when every second was crucial and my concern now seemed hypocritical, but the truth was I had *at last* begun to think practically.

"Lie there," I said to Hugo, who was feebly vomiting slime and muddy water. "Hold onto this rope and *don't* let go."

I thrust the knotted end of rope into his hands and entered the water, the other end of rope tied with a double nelson round my waist. Inhaling deeply I then pushed myself down, my hands exploring the metal wall for the telltale bolts of the ladder. But I must have invented it - goodness knows I seemed to have invented enough silly things from that era. Even after several descents to the left and right of my original spot I found nothing. No ladder, no sunken barge.

Perhaps I should not berate myself excessively because it took the emergency services a long hour to locate the boat and winch it clear of the water, using specialist equipment and an experienced rescue team - and still no body to be found. Eventually they discovered her lying near the pillar supporting the arched bridge, so she must have fallen overboard immediately the boat sank. The pole was stuck deep in the mud and lay across her, pinning her down.

Perhaps we should have thought to look for the pole instead of the boat, but at a depth of five and a half meters I don't imagine we would have found it. Perhaps though, if one honestly wants to look for what might have prevented the whole tragedy, we never should have gone to visit her in the first place.

Sometimes, even now, it comes back to me. On restless nights when I cannot sleep I suddenly rear awake in a cold sweat, my galloping thoughts plagued by guilt.

I should never have gone there. My motives were selfish. It was only because our sick car needed a rest, not a genuine urge to rekindle a past friendship. And I should have tried to contact Alice the moment I realised her mind was wandering, that she was in no fit state to live alone. Or, I should have tried to steer her back to reality, not encouraged her fantasies of living in the past, being young again, capable and strong, and having a boat that was still canal-worthy.

Hugo tries very hard to reason me out of this guilt-ridden state, to suggest a more positive perspective.

"How can you possibly blame yourself? You did *nothing* wrong! If Alice had cared two hoots about her aunt she wouldn't have neglected her all those years. She didn't even bother to go her funeral, for God's sake! Listen Chloe, Trudy *enjoyed* her evening with us. You know she did; it was probably the most fun she'd had in years. And if anyone had known how senile she really was she'd have been thrust into an Old People's home - and hated it. Perhaps what happened was all for the best."

Hugo's words always comfort me and I know what he says is true. But somewhere in my subconscious I still feel guilty. Not for what happened on that final morning; that I *can* now see was not really my responsibility. The guilt is more for the lack of understanding I showed when I was fourteen, for giggling secretly with Alice over our mutual portrait of her as a prim, sexless, childless woman who epitomized just the type of repressed woman we never wanted to become.

And we laughed at Uncle Rob too because we knew he was sexually frustrated - but perhaps all he really wanted was a child of his own. I certainly cannot be sure her interpretation of a 'mean' Rob and their seemingly unpleasant relationship was truthful that last night, not considering all the other ways her mind was distorting reality.

I suppose if the whole tragic experience taught me anything at all, it was that we do not know other people like we think we do.

Drizzle

A fine drizzle hung in the air like sauna steam, but far from being pleasantly warm it was ice cold and permeated everything with its sodden, drenching dampness. The tall grasses, after bravely surviving a month of autumn gales and early frosts, suddenly lost the will to live. They keeled over in a perfectly synchronised swoon to drown themselves in mud.

At the same time - but in the opposite direction - little clusters of buff coloured mushrooms sprouted with the speed of an allergy rash from the mulch of autumn leaves beneath the birch trees. And the pungent smell of mildew oozed from everywhere. There was not the faintest breath of wind yet the heavy, downward pressure of moist air created a strange, eerie whispering sound - like a ghostly choir.

A long-haired mongrel nosed along the waterlogged ditch which divided the fields from the narrow strip of woodland. It was large enough to be mistaken for a wolf through the indistinct veil of drizzle, but its demeanour was too humble and skulking for it to be a serious predator. All the same it seemed to fool the roosting birds that it posed a danger, for they began to squawk hysterically.

Several yards behind it trudged a gaunt man in a dripping raincoat, his hair plastered wetly against his skull, his collar flicked up and his shoulders hunched in a hopeless attempt to divert the rivulet of cold water which trickled down his spine. Part of him resisted the cold discomfort (the seams of his boots had also let in water and squelched with every step), while part welcomed it - because, the way he was currently feeling, it made no sense him still being alive *unless* he suffered.

He followed the dog along the hedgerow. But whereas it eagerly noticed the shrew scurrying into the bole of the old oak tree, gleefully eyed the linnet fluttering nervously overhead, and happily breathed in all the exciting new smells of wet earth and fermentation, he took no notice of his surroundings, being fully encased in a private thought-world of his own gloomy making.

It was only when he accidentally slithered down the pathway leading to the kitchen door at the back of the cottage that he paid any attention to where he placed his feet. It was a waterslide now amd as slippery as an eel-skin; if he blundered blindly down it he would end up on his backside - and in his current fragile state he had to be extra careful not to fall at all.

The moment he opened the door the dog bolted in and flung itself onto the hearthrug in front of the kitchen range, as if in a mad race to beat a pack of snarling, rival dogs for this, the warmest, cosiest spot in the house. A faint shadow of a smile at last flitted across his face as he acknowledged that the dog - just like him - seemed so ready to delude itself that its life was one of jostling, cheery companionship, not the solitary one it was in reality. He could remember the first time he had brought it here in a little cardboard box lined with straw, when it was a plump, wriggling puppy just seven weeks old. From then on it had never shared its space with any other dog, so it ought surely to have known by now that it lived alone. Whereas his situation…well, he still had the evidence propped on ledges and shelves: photos, trinkets, cards, ornaments, mementos, all gazing down at him, reminding him of his family.

He hung his dripping raincoat over the rush doormat and, limping wearily, plodded in wet socks to the tomblike chill of the larder, which was colder than any conventional fridge, to fetch root vegetables for a warming soup. Then he peeled, chopped and grated, happy to keep his hands busy and his mind distracted, so that by the time he was ready to lay the table he need not question why he laid more than one bowl, for by then it would seem natural.

When the vegetables were soft enough to be impaled on a fork he carried the tureen to the table and watched the steam spiral upwards, noticing how the windows had misted over, and how the air now wept moisture inside and out.

Today, however, he uncharacteristically helped himself first. Then his hand hesitated for several seconds with the ladle brimful - and did *not* pour it into the second bowl. He had been helping her to food religiously every day; but suddenly today he had stopped! Nor did he butter the slice of bread he had cut for her, the crusty end slice that she loved to nibble at. The dog must have noticed the change too - either that or it was fondly dreaming of chasing rabbits in and out of warrens, for its tail thumped rhythmically on the tiled floor and it whimpered excitedly.

He was tempted to offer her the cheese first, because yesterday he had hacked at it and she would deftly restore it to a more civilised shape… But again he managed to resist the urge.

"I might *even* make ends meet financially," he told himself, "if I start to buy and cook only for myself." And, much as he hated the heartless practicality of such a statement he applauded it for one aspect - that it at last looked forwards into the future instead of mournfully back at the past.

The telephone rang, instantly catapulting the dog out of its mellow dream into a panic of alertness - claws scraping the tiles after gouging ugly gaping holes in the rug, banging its head clumsily against a table leg, scrambling to the door, scratching and whining frenziedly. He, however, did not move a muscle. He knew it was only his mother making her routine check-up call, and if he did not answer her now she would ring again in an hour. He would be able to handle it better by then. And there was no harm ignoring it, for she would not seriously worry unless he missed several calls.

She had stayed with him for his first week back at the cottage, to cushion the blow and ease the transition. But it was obvious throughout that she was edgy and itching to get back to her own life.

"You *sure* you'll be alright?" she had asked him fifty times over as she wrapped her duffle coat around her spindly frame prior to departure, and hunted for her gloves - which the dog had buried in its basket after chewing off both thumbs. It had spent the long period of his hospitalisation at her house, and unfairly repaid her kindness by perversely gnawing at - or gobbling up - all her valuables. "I'll call every day, for the first bit anyway. You can always stay with me, you know, if it's truly *too* difficult."

He had nodded but knew he would not. He *had* to learn to cope. Had already stolen more than enough of everyone's concern, attention and sympathy over the last few months until he could sense they had reached a point of utter exhaustion with him and his plight. Eventually even the kindest, most unselfish person resents someone who is a perpetual drain on their spirits.

Relating to the emotional drama at the beginning must have been easier. When his survival was touch and go and he was on life support; then later too - when he looked likelier to survive but remained in an induced coma, and they still suspected irreversible brain damage. Then, no doubt, both sets of relatives were harmoniously united in hoping and praying he would recover.

In emergencies people tend to pull together and focus on healthy, positive thinking. For a short period, anyway.

He could imagine his mother sitting patiently beside his inert body, (leafing through her magazines and snipping out the adverts for cut price conservatories, no doubt). Hoping, as she snipped away, that he would soon recover his ability to think, feel, move, and ultimately lead an independent life. But she must surely have also weighed up the advantages (somewhat guiltily of course) of him remaining a vegetable and therefore dependent on her, with the counterbalancing benefit of hefty compensation so that she could afford a luxury conservatory; or (more sensibly perhaps) a whole new, larger house altogether!

He wondered whether it occurred to her then that he might recover *physically*, yet still stay psychologically and emotionally scarred.

Of course he, too, had passed through progressive stages of recovery after regaining consciousness. At first he remembered nothing. Not just of the attack, but of several weeks before it happened; and then of course nothing at all of the weeks while he lay in a coma afterwards. Unconsciousness - *that* had been a simple state. Oblivious of the police investigation going on around him, unaware of their forensic examinations of him - even as they fought to keep him alive, so that they could either mount evidence against him - or eliminate him as a suspect.

Though how he could *possibly* have battered his own head with such force was, surely, stretching credulity.

When they did eventually break the news to him once he had recovered consciousness, even though by then they had an extensive casefile on the attack and a half-way feasible profile on its possible perpetrators (a so-called 'drug gang' from the town - but little solid evidence to cement a case against them, nor any obvious motive beyond mindless, drug-induced violence) the drift of their questioning still hinted that he might not have defended his family as a husband should. *Perhaps*, they appeared to suggest (when he was well enough to communicate what little he remembered), he had given undue priority to saving his own skin. Or had he only imagined this muted criticism because he continuously levelled it at himself, or sometimes absorbed it in the thinly veiled vitriol behind many of Natalie's parents' remarks?

The police officer who told him the sad details: that Rowan had clung to life for five more hours after their bodies were found by another walker, but

Natalie and Katie were already dead, even before the ambulance men arrived to stretcher all four bodies through the closely growing trees to the ambulance, had been a different breed of policeman. Sensitive, carefully trained, a specialist in delivering tragic news to family members. His own feelings of guilt at being the sole survivor were apparently an absolutely standard reaction - or so this policeman assured him. And the hospital psychiatrist also battled to persuade him of it. Also, he did understand that detectives in a murder investigation always suspect those who are closest to the victims first, and four out of five times they are right.

He had found it easier to accept their deaths whilst still in hospital. One is somehow conditioned to expect death there. Also, he was cocooned and cosseted, treated like a delicate child or alternatively, ridiculously, some kind of heroic character, perpetually fed the idea that it was a sheer miracle he had managed to survive so he *must* make the most of it. The routine, the constant attention, the whole momentum of their charted parabola for his recovery - all of it helped keep him occupied. He had tried to stay positive for others' sakes. And the drugs they give you after a head injury numb the brain anyway.

He had known it would be painfully difficult coming back to the cottage. Natalie's parents had tidied away all the rawest signs of family life; all the little things kids leave heaped on floors or trailing out of drawers and cupboards, when they play full-tilt and are interrupted mid-game, and fully expect to be back in half an hour to carry on where they left off. It was only meant to be a quick trip to the woods, after all…

Now, nearly everything meaningful or personal had vanished and the curtain brought emphatically down on that last day. The cottage was so sanitised it looked almost as impersonal as a holiday let. The children's bedroom had been emptied, repainted, reassembled as an office. But whether they had contrived this total 'disappearance' of all their belongings to spare him more agony, or had deliberately, spitefully, deprived him of the right to hold onto the memory of their grandchildren, he could not be sure.

At least they had left him *some* traces of Natalie. A few of her less worn clothes hung forlornly in the cupboard, most of her private papers were still tucked away in her desk, and hardly any of the photographs - except his very favourite ones of her - had gone from the kitchen mantelpiece.

Yet the fact that her underwear, her toiletries and many of her personal possessions (and all her childhood ones) had gone gave him the strangest feeling. Had the hospital psychiatrist suggested it? Or did it come from mistaken kindness, to lessen his pain by diluting his intimate memories? (Or perhaps prevent him being able to relive them in some unhealthy, aberrational manner?) Or, was it simply to deprive him of her, a vindictive *quid pro quo* for him having deprived them...?

He could not honestly resent their blaming him when he constantly blamed himself. He *should* have sacrificed himself to defend his young family. The only possible excuse for not doing so was if he had been attacked first; otherwise the blows to the back and side of his head did suggest he had been running away. And the fact that he was the only witness yet could remember nothing at all, well it must look - to an unsympathetic observer anyway - suspicious.

One of the terrible downsides to the partial recovery of his memory was that he now, all-too-frequently, relived the horrific sounds and confusing motions of the attack, and it was always the relentless wailing of the ambulance siren that woke him up from his nightmare. Yet only these disembodied sounds returned, nothing visual at all. He still had no idea what the attackers looked like and would not be able to positively identify them, should it come to trial.

His mother would be phoning again in twenty minutes. This time he must take her call or she would worry. Reluctantly he brushed aside his reverie and stood up to clear away the scattering of bread crumbs and the two soup bowls. She would find it 'disturbed' that he cooked for Natalie and talked to her whilst 'they' ate, talked to her quite often in fact as he moved around the house. But he never talked to the children. He wondered why not - because he could still picture them with exquisite clarity. In fact if he stared at the smouldering fire he could see them clearly right now, hunched over their Ludo board, prising the red counters out of the thick pile carpet and giggling conspiratorially at the habitual silliness of the dog who lay fast asleep *again*, its hairy belly heaving up and down like the sea at high tide, dribbling slimily onto its forepaws. Was this a genuine memory, perhaps even from that last day before the walk? Or was it merely his imagination playing tricks?

He heard them too. Sometimes he could distinctly hear their running footsteps on the stairs, or the muffled thuds as they gleefully tobogganed down them, and it would bring the flicker of a smile to his face. It was purely a trick of memory, like a shadow, and he had begun to suspect that love and memory were linked - and that his drugs suppressed them both. So today he had taken no drugs, steeled himself to eat alone without Natalie, and forced himself to walk to the outskirts of those fateful woods. It was a minor breakthrough.

Suddenly he was wrenched from these thoughts by obstreperous banging on the front door. Old oak country doors have no convenient peepholes to pre-warn of visitors and he assumed it must be his mother, returned to appease her fledgeling worries and simultaneously retrieve the reading glasses she had left behind. Otherwise he would never have opened the door…

On the doorstep stood a girl of around fourteen or fifteen wearing patched jeans and a dripping woollen jacket. She was nervously twiddling a broken rainbow-striped umbrella that kept her head dry but funnelled the rain like a gargoyle's gaping spout straight onto her left shoulder.

"I'm sorry calling on you like this, out of the blue," she said, noting his distinct lack of welcome, "but I need to talk to you. Just for a minute."

He hesitated. "OK," he eventually agreed, and the dog growled menacingly.

"Smart dog." She sighed, "They always pick up on things we don't."

Rather presumptuously she hung her dripping jacket next to his weeping raincoat, and the rain pattered off them to different rhythms, hers having the faster, bouncier tempo. He limped over to his seat in the fireside armchair, vaguely gesturing to her that she could sit wherever she wished.

"So, what is it you want?" he asked, acutely conscious of his slurred speech. Up until now he had not spoken to anyone unaware of his condition who would not understand the immense effort it cost him to even wrap his tongue around words at all - let alone pronounce them halfway properly.

"Miserable weather," she complained, completely ignoring his question, "and it's *so* incredibly dark in here - I can't hardly see a thing."

Her accusatory tone annoyed him. He did not know her (as far as he could remember), and she was unlikely to be a near neighbour because his mother had expressly asked them all to leave him be - explaining he would call on them once he felt ready. Why *had* he invited her in?

"It's intentionally dark," he answered tersely. "Lights give me a headache - and the same with too much talking."

"Oh I'm sorry," she said, suddenly contrite. "I didn't mean it rudely. I *do* know about your injuries." She glanced at the rain driving horizontally against the window pane and gave an instinctive shudder, as if she doubted the efficacy of the protective shield of the glass. "It's what I came about."

"Excuse me?" Because of the constant sizzling noise in his ears he sometimes misheard the simplest of things.

Her eyes flitted nervously back to the window and her voice sank to a whisper, "I know… who did it." She swivelled round towards the window again as if terrified someone might be lurking in the back garden, eavesdropping on them.

His hands jerked upwards convulsively, but he managed to control them by gripping onto the arm of his chair. "Get out!" he sputtered furiously, "What sort of a sick, twisted joke...? Get out *now* - before I call the police. If you *really* knew something you'd have gone straight to them."

He tried to stand up so as to forcibly shepherd her out but his legs refused to support his weight, despite the feather-lightness of his skeletal body. The dog raised its hackles and bared its teeth, growling aggressively. Her jaunty confidence immediately evaporated and she shrank into the far corner of the room.

"Call it off me!" she wailed, "I got mauled by an alsation once when I was little. I've never trusted dogs since."

He whistled softly and the dog's aggression subsided. He found it mildly comforting that it still felt some sort of protective loyalty to him, because it had always been Natalie's dog more than his or the childrens'. His head began to pound and each reverberation hammered more persistently. It was now clear that his decision not to take the powerful anti-inflammatory drugs that morning - in total disregard of all medical advice - severely disadvantaged him, since there was far more risk of him having a seizure or black out.

Still, he decided, if she *had* brought back-up and they were hiding in the garden waiting for the right moment to break in, he would anyway have been a pathetically easy prey, drugs or no drugs. And the dog was no real match for thugs with hammers either, that fact had sadly been proved already. Infinitely slowly he groped for his phone.

"Don't be so bloody daft," she said quickly, "if I'd gone to the police I'd be dead - else of course I'd have told them already. Think about it - even if I do get them arrested, they'll still get me killed if they find out who grassed."

He studied her dizzily. Her eyes were a pale, milky blue and stared blankly back at him, unwavering. They could just as easily be honest as crazily neurotic. The finger nails on her left hand were savagely bitten to the quick, but nervousness can be triggered by many things. Her mouth, of all her features the most appealing, was asymmetrical because of a faint, almost imperceptible muscle spasm on one side. The sign of a liar? A fantasist? Or had his own feeling of vertigo merely *invented* the twitching?

He could not easily read her, but he sensed that her motives were nothing to do with the pursuit of justice. So, for the moment he stalled, unsure of his next move, or whether he was capable of one.

"You've got proof I take it," his voice was surprisingly steadier, "not just wild allegations."

"'Course I do. But first you've got to bloody *swear* you'll never say it came from me."

"Why should I promise anything to someone I don't even know?"

"Well, I do...*did*...know your wife."

She seemed now to be staring at the family photos on the mantelpiece behind him, hoping to find Natalie there. Yet her eyes were unfocused - as if gazing at something beyond the limits of visibility. Perhaps it *was* the classic stare of insanity.

He was momentarily distracted by a confusion of sounds as his ears fluttered and crackled from the rapid drumming of the rain on the window sill, which kept uncannily perfect time with the urgent beating of his heart. She shifted her weight onto her other leg, still nervously hugging the far corner of the room, absentmindedly stroking the tassels of the newly hung brocade curtains Natalie's mother had imposed upon him.

"My little brother was in her class at St.Aidan's Primary - as was the kid sister of one of them that did it. *That's* why it happened, if you want to know." Her injured tone accused him of unfairly not believing her after the immense leap of courage it had taken her to come and divulge such dangerous secrets. "She only went and confiscated Tammy's mobile phone, didn't she? *Big* mistake."

He had no idea, so although his lips moved this time as if he were trying to talk, perhaps express bewilderment that such a minor action on Natalie's part had led to any repercussion, he still said nothing.

"Well then, that's why. 'She had it coming', didn't she? That's how those scumbags think - *and* the gang of male-trash that hang around with them, not having brains of their own with which to think differently. *I* should know, I've been in the same class as them since Primary - and that was years before your wife showed up. And if you think I'm only grassing just to pay them back," she noticed that his eyes were questioning the three concentric red wheals around her wrist, "then you're every bit as stupid as your wife."

His neck ached and his head felt swollen to twice its normal size. He swayed to and fro in his chair like a pendulum, longing to lie down, close his eyes and go to sleep. He should never have walked such a distance that morning, after the numerous times he had been told to build up to things gradually or invite a setback; compounded by omitting the drugs. The room grew *much* darker all of a sudden, but perhaps that was only due to the general gloominess of a rainy November afternoon.

With sudden, ear-piercing abruptness a car horn hooted impatiently from the road. He winced at the shrill sound, wondering if this was the long-awaited signal that violent reinforcements had finally arrived. However she looked equally startled.

"Me dad," she said, her eyes flickering towards his oak entrance door. "It means I've got to go. I told him I was only bringing you this condolence card from the kids in Natalie's Class." She scurried to her still-dripping jacket and drew a huge handmade envelope out of the pocket on the drier side - although it was still blotched and soggy. "Here it is." She thrust it hurriedly into his thin, trembling hands. "The happy slap photos are inside the card. Not very clear, but clear enough to recognise two or three of their ugly mugs."

And she hurried away without giving him a backward glance, banging the door shut behind her and forgetting her broken rainbow umbrella.

He heaved himself unsteadily to his feet and hobbled to the window just in time to catch a glimpse of the car as it accelerated away towards the main road. His vision was too impaired to decipher any part of its registration number, but he recognised significant other details: it was an old, emerald green Vauxhall Corsair with a huge dent in the offside rear door and no hubcaps. Moreover its driver was barely out of his teens, so way too young to be her father.

At first the feeling of nausea and aftershock was nearly overwhelming, but after clinging to the banister rail at the foot of the stairs he eventually managed to struggle back to the living room. It was ridiculous how weak and wasted his muscles had become after so many months in a hospital bed, and how sluggishly and dully his brain functioned. He still did not seem to understand who she was, why she had come, or what sort of a sick, practical joke might have been slipped into that envelope.

He first contemplated throwing it on the fire without bothering to inspect it, but by the time he reached the room the dog had already pre-empted him. It had not hurled it on the flames of course, but had applied its own, well-practised method of chewing the thing into slobbery pieces.

"Oh well," he gave a faint shrug, "at least I'm spared knowing."

It was in fact better not to know, he now convinced himself. Better to learn to forget. Those who think punishment brings closure and relief for victims are not necessarily right, and anyway, he disapproved of the whole idea of retribution. Nothing could bring Natalie and the children back. And if it were really true that they had died due to an act of such disproportionately brutal revenge, then knowing that would not help at all. He would feel such bitterness. The dog had eaten wisely this time.

But then he noticed his mother's half-chewed leather glove thumbs protruding from the cushion, and remembered that she must be on the verge of calling him again. Fifteen minutes must have passed - she would call within the next five. He hunted for his phone - and eventually found it on the fireside table where he had placed it when he threatened to contact the police. Incredibly, he had not been quite as slow-witted as he had assumed. It was still on and in *record* mode. He listened back, and found to his amazement that every single word of their conversation had been faithfully preserved.

"I can't have it both ways," he now decided. "First I assume fate's destroyed the evidence so that must be for the best; but now that it's been saved I'll have to go along with that. I *have* to take the responsibility. Otherwise they'll kill someone else."

He dialled his mother's number and his finger scarcely trembled.

"Hi. No. I'm alright, it's just that you've left your reading glasses here, and there's something important I want to tell you. Fine, fine - I'll expect you here in an hour."

He could relax now, knowing that his mother would handle it efficiently. She anyway had a much more comfortable relationship with the police than he did.

He sat for a long time gazing out on the rain soaked garden, watching the parallel lines of raindrops as they slid down the window pane like the threads of a bead curtain hung with tiny glinting pearls. This rain had been a long, long time coming, and the parched earth greedily drank it in.

In some curiously empathetic way he felt that the steady rain seemed also to nourish his own shrivelled and dessicated soul, reinvigorating all the pent-up feelings that he - or his drugs - had for so long suppressed. But it nevertheless surprised him when he brushed his cheek with his hand to find it was soaking wet with tears. He had not cried once, not throughout all those months. Now he seemed absolutely powerless to stop.